I TEMPORARILY DO

A ROMANTIC COMEDY

ELLIE CAHILL

ALSO BY ELLIE CAHILL

When Joss Met Matt

Call Me, Maybe

Just a Girl

AS LIZ CZUKAS

Ask Again Later

Top Ten Clues You're Clueless

Throwing My Life Away

ISBN-13: 978-1974477425

～

For Lees and Amanda

WORST. DAY. EVER

he guys were all in the living room. No lights except from the glow of the TV. The noises coming from the room told me they were virtually killing a bunch of other gamers in another room that probably looked a lot like this one. Dark, noisy with smack talk, and fueled by most of a case of beer.

I wasn't in the mood for any of it. And frankly, I didn't want them to see me like this. Tears dried in tracks down my cheeks, eyes red and puffy. Even with my big sunglasses on, I was sure it was obvious that I was a hot mess. And I had every right to be. This was the kind of distress that called for sympathy from my girls.

Don't get me wrong, my guy roommates had their advantages. Sometime it was way easier to take the beer they offered, flop down on the couch and cheer along with them to whatever University sport they'd managed to find on TV. Distracting, escapist fun. That had its time and place.

Now was not that time.

So I didn't even say hello as I headed up the stairs to take refuge in the room I shared with Ashley. She wasn't in there, though. And my other female roommate, Mary, wasn't in her room down the hall.

Where were my girls in my time of need? Didn't they know I was having literally the worst day of my life?

Frustrated tears sprung to my eyes afresh and I forgot I was still wearing my sunglasses when I tried to wipe them away, instead shoving the frames further into my face. Which was totally in keeping with the rest of my day. I yanked the glasses off angrily and tossed them on my bed.

Footsteps came up the stairs and I hurried to the doorway, hoping it was Ashley or Mary. But the tread was too heavy, I realized. It had to be one of the guys.

I tried to duck back into my room and close the door, but I was spotted.

"Em?" It was Beckett, looking surprised to see me. "Didn't hear you come in."

I gave an over-exaggerated shrug. "I'm home."

"Yeah." He didn't seem himself. His posture was heavy and his voice didn't have its usually upbeat inflection. Beckett had surfer looks, with his light brown hair and blue eyes, and a buoyant, laid back personality to match. The Beckett I was seeing before me was not the Beckett I was used to.

"Do you—" I paused for a breath, trying to prevent any telltale squeaks from giving away my mental state. "Do you know where the girls are?"

Beckett looked around almost surprised. "No. I just came up to use the bathroom…"

"Don't let me stop you." I gestured toward one of the two bathrooms on this floor. Our townhouse-style apartment was a narrow tower of rooms, with two bedrooms on each of the second and third floors, but the bathrooms were weirdly both on the middle floor, right next to each other. The girls had staked out one as a group, while the guys were left to their own devices in the other. As a rule, I avoided theirs. The cleanliness level was considerably lower and you never knew if you were going to step on a wet towel or just some unidentifiable puddle.

Beckett started toward his bathroom, but paused to give me another look. "You all right?"

My lips twitched, as if they were trying to tell him the whole story without my brain's permission. But I managed to contain myself and gave him a nod. "Sure."

He seemed uncertain, but trudged to the bathroom without further comment.

From the living room below, I heard the sound of a group shout from Brady and Jake. They were apparently playing on without Beckett. Which was kind of weird. Usually any bathroom breaks were accompanied by continuing impatient cries from the other players while they suffered through the horrors of Pause.

I went back into my room and sank down on the bed, just missing crushing my abandoned sunglasses. Sitting was pretty much the only thing I could think of to do.

I was utterly and completely tapped out. Reserve tanks empty.

Which is how Beckett found me staring into space when he emerged from the bathroom. He paused in the door to my dark room.

"You sure you're okay?"

I had to tell someone. "I have had the worst day. Ever."

"Not worse than mine," he said softly.

"You have no idea."

"No, *you* have no idea."

"Trust me, there is no way yours was worse." My voice cracked on the last word.

He reached into his pocket and emerged with a five-dollar bill, which he held out to me. "Five bucks says it was." Beckett and the other guys were always willing to make a wager with whatever happened to be in their pockets.

"Yeah, see, I don't even have five bucks to make that bet with."

Now his face creased with concern. "Emmy, what happened?"

"I don't even know where to begin." I pressed the heels of my hands into my eyes for a second, before ticking off the points on my fingers. "Basically I'm completely screwed for the fall."

In less than a week, our lease was up on this quirky townhouse. In fact, my lease was up on life as I knew it. The six of us were college grads now. Real life was supposed to be on the horizon.

But not for me. Not anymore.

"What do you mean?" Beckett asked.

"You remember I found that roommate on Craigslist?"

"Yeah. What's-her-name…uh, Bonnie something?"

"Yeah, well…" I gave another exaggerated shrug. "Maybe the name should have been a clue. Like Bonnie and Clyde." At this point, a hiccuping sob burst out of me, and Beckett sank onto my bed beside me.

The sickening crunch of failing plastic told me he'd sat right on my sunglasses.

He jumped up in surprise, revealing the completely destroyed frames and the lenses both popped out.

"Oh shit!" he said. "I'm sorry, I didn't—"

I cut him off with a wave of my hand. "It's fine. It doesn't even matter."

"I'll replace them."

"Forget it."

"Em, what is going on?"

I did finger-quotes around her name, "*Bonnie* kited a bunch of checks from my account. Then, she disappeared. Oh, but that wasn't enough, oh no. She completely overdrafted my account, *and* she never even paid the security deposit. I'm not even sure there *was* a lease." My chin quivered violently for a moment and my face threatened to crumple, but I seized control of myself. "I don't even have what I need for my tuition payment next month. I'm broke. I'm homeless and I don't know where I'm going to go!

I don't even—" The last word disappeared in a high pitched wail as my last shred of self-control faded.

Beck didn't speak, just came to the other side of me, half-sitting on my pillow and put an arm around my shoulders. Now my angry bravado disappeared completely and I gave in to helpless, broken crying. One, two, and half of a third sob, before I pressed the fingertips of one hand between my eyebrows. Was it supposed to be some kind of off switch? I wasn't sure, but it didn't seem to work.

"What am I going to do?" I squeaked.

"We'll figure it out," he said soothingly. "Did you call the police?"

I nodded, sniffling. "Yeah, but they didn't sound real confident they'd catch her."

Beckett inhaled like he was going to say something, but he either didn't have anything to say after all, or thought better of it. Instead, he just tightened his arm around me reassuringly.

"Damn it." Now my fingertips moved to the hollows below my eyes. Was there a chakra for not crying? Some kind of acupressure thing I should learn?

We sat together in the quiet room for a few minutes, not talking. The only sound was my occasional sniffles as I faded from the immediacy of my personal disaster to a state more like numbness. It wasn't any more helpful as emotional states went, but at least it didn't involve so much snot.

When the well was dry, I asked, "So, do I even need to ask if I won the bet?"

"That really was a shitty day."

"The worst."

"Pretty bad."

"Oh please. What could possibly be any worse than getting all your money stolen and being homeless?"

"Emily left me."

"Wait, what?" I demanded.

5

"Yep," he sighed.

"Emily? Your fiancée, Emily?"

"That's the one."

"But—you're getting married, like, next week!"

Beckett shook his head. "Not anymore."

"Why?!" My own problems forgotten, I looked at him with wide eyes. "How did—what? Why?"

Beckett didn't answer, instead leaning away from me to pull out his phone. He tapped into his email and held it out for me to read.

Dear Beckett,

This is the hardest letter I've ever had to write. I know I should do this in person, but I just can't look at your face while I do this. We're rushing things, and I need to slow down. Getting married just for a place in university housing is no reason to make such a commitment. We're both so young. I'm not even done with my undergrad degree yet. And switching schools at this point feels wrong for me. Even if it would mean we'd finally be together.

I hope you can understand why I'm calling it off. I hope you can forgive me for not having the nerve to say it in person. I need some time to think right now. We're just too young.

I've loved you for so long, I don't even know what it's like to be without you. I can't help wondering if we're only doing this because it's the Next Thing. And that's no reason to get married.

I know you'll support this decision, because I know you love me enough to do what's best for both of us.

I can't marry you.

I'm sorry.

- Emily

"HOLY—" the word came out of me in a gasp.

"Yeah."

"Oh my god, Beckett." I threw my arms around his waist, squeezing him in a tight hug. "I'm so sorry!"

"Yeah," he said flatly.

"How can she—what about—isn't she—" I couldn't even get my thoughts straight enough to figure out where to start with my questions.

"You know what I know." Beckett shrugged.

"Did you reply? Call her? What did she say?"

"I called," he said softly. "But her sister answered. Emily wouldn't come to the phone."

"What did her sister say?"

"Mostly just repeated what was in the email. A lot about rushing things."

"But you guys have been together since high school!" Beckett and Emily were an institution as far as I was concerned. Sure, Emily went to school in Arizona, but she was practically an invisible 7th roommate in our house. She was the ghost in every conversation. The constant in Beckett's plans for the future.

"I know."

I felt like I was suddenly in a foreign country where I didn't speak the language. A world without my stalwart friend and roommate getting married next week was a world I did not recognize.

See, Beckett and Emily had a plan. Emily was transferring schools to spend the last year of her undergrad career at the same school where Beckett—and I—were going to grad school. They were going to live in the same city for the first time since high school. They were going to live in the same apartment for the first time ever.

The only wrench in the system? Emily's conservative parents didn't want her living with her boyfriend before marriage. Never mind the fact that they'd been together for more than five years at this point. Never mind that they were already talking about forever.

But Beckett was even willing to concede on that front. He'd asked Emily to marry him over winter break, and when even that wasn't enough to get her parents to ease up on their concerns, they'd agreed to a simple ceremony before moving in together. Emily still wanted a big white wedding, but they figured that could wait until she graduated. In the meantime, they'd have a quick, quiet wedding and live together as husband and wife.

Maybe it wasn't a fairytale come true, but it seemed like a good compromise for them. And it didn't surprise any of us who knew Beckett. He was the kind of guy you could count on. And we all knew he'd do anything for Emily. As far as I was concerned, they'd been married since the day they met, and it wasn't my business when they tied the knot.

Now this? I couldn't make sense of it. Emily thought they were rushing things?

"But it's her parents' dumb rules that's the reason you guys were getting married in the first place."

"I know," he said, still talking in that flat tone. He was clearly in shock.

"So why doesn't she just tell them to stuff it, and you guys can live together anyway? Who cares what they think?"

"Emily cares. And they pay her bills."

"They'll get over it. There's no way they'd want her to rush into getting married if she's not ready. They'll understand."

"She doesn't want to live with me. She doesn't want any of it."

"You don't know that—"

"Her sister made it pretty clear."

"Oh god, Beck." I hugged him again. "I'm so sorry."

"Thanks." He gave me a half-hearted squeeze in return.

"Is it too early to say that she's a bitch?"

He winced. "Yeah."

"Okay, then I won't." Even though I was thinking it so hard

I'm sure Emily could feel it all the way in her parents' house in Arizona. "Let me know if you change your mind."

"You'll be the first."

"So, I guess you might get to keep your five dollars after all."

"Actually, you'd have to give me five dollars. That's how a bet works."

"Do you want to see the balance of my bank account? I have literally negative dollars right now. I would have to borrow money to have zero dollars."

"Fuckin' A, Emmy." Beckett sighed.

"But if it helps, you win."

"I don't know. I might have gotten stood up at the fucking altar, but at least she didn't clean me out."

"Jesus."

Beckett patted me on the thigh. "Wanna get drunk?"

"I can't afford to go out anywhere. I can't afford to *think* about going out."

"I got a bottle of vodka in the freezer with our names on it."

"What are we drinking it with?"

"Who cares? We'll find something. We gotta empty the fridge before Friday, anyway, right?"

I gave him a little smile. "This feels like a bad decision I can get behind."

BAD DECISIONS R US

*B*rady and Jake were totally on board with our plan to get blitzed. It never took much to convince them to tie one on. And with the added bonus of a reason to drink, it was on.

They even decided to pool their cash and head down the street to the liquor store and contribute a case or two of beer.

Why the hell not? I figured. It's not like I had a lot of options at this point. I had to wait until Monday for the bank to open before I could even hope to get someone to help me with my accounts. I had no cash. I was totally dependent on my friends to even provide me with food for the weekend. Not that I'd need much food if the amount of beer Brady and Jake returned with was any indication.

Jake called Ashley and Mary, demanding they come home immediately and help us have a final roommate blowout misery party. Mary arrived first with a box of cheap wine hanging from each hand.

"Look, there was a sale!" she announced. "Score!"

I raised my empty shot glass to her as I crammed a bite of pickle into my mouth as a chaser. It was actually a pretty good combination, vodka and pickles, I'd discovered. But there were only a few pickles left. "Welcome to the shit show!" I told her when my mouth was clear.

"Let me catch up." Mary grabbed an Avengers 2 commemorative cup from the cabinet and filled it with the cheap rosé from one of her boxes of wine. The cup was easily a 32-ouncer, but I don't think she filled the whole thing. Hard to be sure, though, as my vision was already getting a bit blurry from the number of icy cold vodka shots I'd chased with pickles.

"I like your style, Mary, you know that?" Brady asked cheerfully as he cracked the top off beer number...something.

Soon Ashley got home to join the fray. She was carrying a paper grocery bag that was obviously heavy.

"Hey guys!" she called as she came in. "I snagged the leftovers from tonight's toast!" Ash worked for a catering company that did weddings, and sometimes she was able to bring home goodies for us. The spoils ranged from uneaten wedding cake, to a single plated steak dinner, to half-poured bottles of wine. She was particularly good at uncorking bottles near the end of dinner and making sure they didn't get emptied.

"Got anything to eat in there?" Jake wondered.

"Nope, sorry. Tonight, the Brut's on me, though." Ash set her bag on the table and pulled out four partial bottles of champagne. They weren't cold, or very fizzy after being open for a few hours, but we didn't care.

"We're gonna have to order pizza," Jake decreed.

"Can anyone spot me?" I asked with a hiccup. "I'm not sure pickles are enough of a dinner."

Mary patted my head and helped me get a long strand of my dark hair free from the corner of my lip where my clumsy fingers kept missing it.

"We got you," Jake assured me.

I knew they did. And it broke my heart. Because these people had been my family for two years. They'd been with me after my

11

mom died during my sophomore year. They'd been there for me every step of the way. And Ashley had been my roommate since our first year in the freshman dorms. This was my tribe. My college support system, and we were all going our separate ways in just a few days!

That realization brought on a fresh flood of emotion that was immediately backed up by a resurgence of the awfulness of my financial status. Less than zero. A police report that would probably never lead to a conviction. And nearly two days before I could begin the terrible process of trying to convince my bank that I needed them to restore my money.

So, I did the obvious thing, I started to cry.

"Oh no!" Ashley gushed, hurrying around the table to hug me. "Poor Emmy! Don't cry!"

"Here," Mary thrust one of the open bottles of champagne at me. "This is for happiness. Drink!"

Sniveling, I took a drink. It was so warm and so flat that I almost spit it out in protest, but Mary looked so pleased with having found a solution that I didn't want to hurt her feelings. I forced down the swallow, and another one after that.

"There you go!" Mary cheered like a mother whose toddler just made tinkle on the potty for the first time. "I knew it would help!"

Mary became pretty motherly when she's drinking. She could always be counted on to hold back someone's hair if they were puking. Or to bring you a glass of water. Well, she'd try anyway. Sometimes she ended up setting the cup down on the floor and taking an impromptu nap before she made it back to you, but it was the thought that counted, don't you think?

Ashley scooped up another bottle of the flat champagne and offered it up in toast. "To things only getting better from here."

"God, they can't get worse, can they?" I moaned.

"To dodging the marriage bullet," Brady added, tipping the end of his beer bottle in Beckett's direction.

"Brady!" Mary chided, throwing a handy plastic spoon at him. The kitchen counter was a chaotic heap of things we had already finished from the refrigerator and plenty of things we hadn't. There was a pattern of pale green rings from all the places we'd set the pickle jar. A spattering of red dots from the jar of maraschino cherries that had lingered in the back of the refrigerator since god knew when. We'd used the plastic spoon to fish out all the cherries. There was a half-empty bag of baby carrots that had gone white with dehydration and an open tub of French onion dip that none of us had bothered to check was still within its freshness date. And there were condiments by the dozen. Mustards, ketchup, ranch dressing, dipping sauces in little plastic containers sent over by the local pizza delivery place.

At one point, Brady had asked how much we would pay him to drink all the garlic butter sauce straight from the small cups, but no one took the bet—it was pretty obvious he'd do it for free if he had a few more beers.

"Hey!" Brady protested. "You said yourself they were rushing into this!" He picked up the spoon and pointed it at Mary.

"I nev—I didn't!" Mary's face turned pink with humiliation as she turned to look at Beckett. "I'm sorry! I didn't mean it!"

Beckett looked at her carefully for a long moment. "You said that?"

Now Jake jumped to Mary's defense. "We all did, dude. Don't pick on Mary."

"You all did?" Beckett looked around in surprise.

I wished with all my heart that I could say that I honestly hadn't thought it. But I would have been lying. Even though I'd always believed that Beckett and Emily were the forever kind of couple, I *had* wondered if it was a little foolish to get married and move in together when they hadn't even lived in the same state for so many years. Still, he was my friend, and I wanted to believe that he knew what was right for himself.

Beckett looked at each one of us in turn, silently demanding a response.

"Dude, I said it to your face," Brady said matter-of-factly.

"Yeah, man, you know we both thought you were giving in to her parents too easily," Jake agreed.

This was a bit of a surprise to me. I mean, Brady and Jake had always razzed Beckett about getting hitched, but it all seemed good-natured. Kind of automatic. Like they were just doing what they were expected to do as his buddies.

Now Beckett turned his attention back to Mary. "I just want you to be happy," she said sincerely, eyes brimming with unshed tears.

"Things could still work out with you guys," Ashley offered lamely. "I mean, just because she needs some time doesn't mean that she's cutting you out of her life, does it?" My roommate turned to me expectantly.

I shook my head, making the room slosh unsteadily. "Don't look at me. What the hell do I know about relationships?"

"So none of you thought this was a good idea," Beckett clarified.

"That doesn't mean we weren't going to support you one-hundred percent!" Mary declared emphatically.

"What the hell, you guys?" he said. "Why didn't you say anything?"

"We did," Brady reminded him. "Remember? I said, 'Hey, man, don't you think you should at least see if there's anything there between you two before you go off and get married?'"

"I think you said, 'What if she's gone psycho since you last saw her?'" Jake supplied.

Now Mary grabbed the spoon from Brady's hand and flung it at Jake.

"Hey! I didn't say it, he did!" Jake pointed at Brady. "It was a quote, Mare!"

"Then throw it at him," Mary instructed.

Jake did.

"None of you were going to try to stop me?" Beckett asked.

No one answered. My alcohol soaked brain told me that hours were passing in silence, though in retrospect, it had to be seconds at most.

"What? Like 'I object!' This is not a movie, Beck." At least I think that's what I said. That's what I meant to say.

"Yeah, man," Brady said. "Sometimes you gotta back your friend up, even if he's being a dumbass."

"Jesus. Thanks a lot, you guys." Beckett slid off the high stool where he'd been perched for hours.

The rest of us exchanged glances as his heavy footsteps went up the stairs.

"Oops," Brady said.

"No, forget that," Jake said. "If he didn't think this was a half-assed plan to begin with, there's nothing any of us could have said that would have shown him the light."

No one spoke for a second, then Mary added, "Maybe we should have tried."

"Maybe," Brady said.

"Should one of us check on him?" Ashley wondered, looking up at the ceiling.

"I'll go." I slid off my own stool, surprised by how unstable the floor felt with my feet on it. "Whoa."

"Maybe I should go," Ashley said. "I'm still sober."

"That's okay. I gotta pee like crazy."

I wobbled my way through the living room to the stairs and held the railing with both hands. The steps looked like a mountain to me, but I hauled myself to the second floor. My instincts told me to look for Beckett, but my bladder had a simple majority, and I followed its vote to the bathroom. The neighboring bathroom door was already closed, making me think Beckett might have had the same problem I did.

I took care of business, not bothering to look at my reflection in the mirror over the sink as I washed my hands. It was too frightening a prospect.

Back out in the hall, I found the guy's bathroom door still closed and I tapped on it a few times.

"Beck?"

There was no answer, and I thought I'd have to do my mountain-climbing routine to the third floor to check his bedroom, but then the door clicked open and Beckett was on the other side, looking about as drunk as I felt.

"Hey," I said. "You shouldn't listen to us. You do what you need to feel happy, okay?"

"I thought I was," he said.

"Oh." Yeah, not a whole lot more to say about that, was there? He'd just had the rug pulled out from under him as far as happiness.

"Fuck," he muttered, slumping against the doorframe.

"Maybe she just has cold feet!" I said excitedly. "She's just nervous."

Beckett pulled his phone out of his pocket again and showed me a picture message from Emily. It was a screenshot of an email from the University of Arizona, showing her class list for the fall semester. "Pretty fucking nervous, wouldn't you say?"

"Oh," I said again.

"How long as she been planning to leave me?" he wondered.

I didn't have an answer. It was hard enough to think normal thoughts right now, much less answer questions like that. Instead, I hiccuped once and a little burp escaped me. "Pickle." I grimaced.

Beckett smiled, just a little. "Emmy, I'm sorry. You've got your own shit to deal with. I shouldn't be acting like such a—"

I put my hand over his mouth. "You're not."

"Thanks," he mumbled against my fingers.

With a little smile of my own, I let my hand fall away from his lips. "Mine is just money. It's not the end of the world." I could hardly believe the words were coming out of my mouth. Just hours before I'd thought it was literally the end of the world. I still didn't have a plan. I didn't know if I'd be able to get any of my money back. I didn't know where I was going to live or if I'd be able to pay my fall tuition. But that felt small compared to what Beckett had lost.

"You're a better friend than me." He pushed off the doorframe and pulled me into a hug. "Thanks."

Feeling emotional, I snuggled into his chest. Beckett was tall and broad-shouldered, which made me feel small and safe in his arms. He rubbed one hand over my back, then smoothed down my hair.

"Don't take this this wrong way, but do you have any idea how long it's been since I had sex?"

I giggled, easing back enough to look up at him. "I had no idea you felt that way."

"I don't," he said sternly. "It just…reminded me."

"What did?"

He grinned, embarrassed. "You're just…all girly."

"I'm not having sex with you," I told him.

"I'm not asking you to."

"Good." I disentangled myself from his embrace and gave him an appraising look. "Been that long, huh?"

"Last time I saw her was July 4th weekend."

"Ouch."

"Yeah." He sighed. "And now…"

"You wanna go out and pick up some random girl tonight?" I suggested.

"No."

"Oh come on. Could be just what you need. Get a little strange."

"I'd be useless."

"You're just out of practice. You'd be fine. Nothing to it. It's like riding a bike. A sexy bike."

17

"Even if I wanted to, I don't think I could."

"Why not?"

"I can't even see straight."

"That's the perfect amount of drunkenness for rebound sex."

He leaned toward me, looking me in the eyes. "It's not happening."

"Oh!" I said with sudden understanding and held up one limp finger. "Whiskey dick?"

"Jesus, Em." But he laughed. "No, okay? Whiskey brain maybe."

I shook my head disapprovingly. "Suit yourself."

"Thank you, I will."

"You're probably used to it by now, eh?" I teased with a grin and the barest darting glance toward the crotch of his shorts.

"Oh fuck you."

"I already said no to that."

"Just as well. You couldn't handle me."

I laughed. "Pretty sure you've got that backwards."

"I guess we'll never know."

"Come on," I tugged on his arm. "Let's go back down and show the others you're okay."

"Okay-ish," he agreed.

"That'll do for now."

BY THE LIGHT OF DAY

$\mathcal{F}$or the record, drinking is not a recommended method for cleaning out your refrigerator.

I woke up on top of my blankets, and Ashley in bed with me. I didn't know if we'd planned this, or she'd somehow gotten lost on the way to her own bed across the room. But we were both mostly dressed, so that was a positive thing.

There was a yellow stain on my best friend's cheek that looked suspiciously like mustard. And a strand of my dark brown hair was stuck to it. How weird had shit gotten last night?

I tied to sit up, but the pounding in my head and the immediate tsunami of nausea pulled me back down to the pillow in record time.

Oh hangover gods, please forgive me. What offering must I make that you might take this cup of suffering from my lips?

I groaned, which made Ashley burrow further into the pillow. "What time is it?" she moaned.

"I'm going to puke," I answered, which was all it took to get her out of my bed as fast as if she'd been beamed up. I lurched to my feet and rushed down the hall to the girls' bathroom, dropping to my knees just in time to dry heave. Nothing came up, but the action made my pounding head feel like someone had set off a bomb beneath my temples.

I moaned and dropped to the cold tile floor, so so happy that I knew it was relatively clean.

Bits of the previous evening played through my mind as I lay there waiting for the room to stop spinning. Something about licking mustard off our fingers instead of salt before tequila shots. Where the hell had the tequila even come from? Standing on the coffee table singing "Party in the U.S.A." with Mary and Ashley. Announcing to all of my roommates that we needed to get Beckett laid ASAP.

I hoped that last part wasn't a real memory.

There had been pizza at some point, if the taste in my mouth was anything to go by. Maybe it had been enough to soak up my stomach contents? Was that why I hadn't actually barfed this morning?

Ugh.

Mary shuffled into the bathroom with a grunt.

"Throw up?" she asked.

"No."

"Gotta pee."

"Can't get up."

"Move over."

I wiggled my body close enough to the tub to give Mary room to use the toilet. That's friendship, people.

She hung her head in her upraised hands while she sat on the toilet. "Gonna die," she said on an exhale.

"Uh huh."

Eventually she got up and washed her hands, then splashed water all over her face. She was sloppy, causing water to spatter down on me where I still curled on the bathmat. Then she nudged me in the butt with one foot until I rolled over enough to accept the little paper cup of water in her hand.

"Thank you," I said.

"Love you," she muttered, shuffling back out of the room, and turning the lights off on me as she went.

An hour later, I woke up, still on the floor, with my small cup of water spilled all over the front of my shirt.

This was definitely a hangover for the record books. My body ached miserably from the cold floor. So I managed to pull myself up, stopping at the sink to stick my mouth under the running faucet and get as much hydration as I thought I could handle. This was no job for Dixie cups.

On my way back to the bedroom I shared with Ashley, I couldn't help noticing that Mary had left her own door hanging open. Her room was tiny—the price of having the single room—so the bed was clearly visible from the door. Although they were buried under the blankets, it was obvious that Mary wasn't the only person in her bed.

My eyebrows went up, the fog of hangover clearing a bit. What exactly had gone on last night?

Back in our room, I discovered Ashley had moved to her own bed, though she was still on top of the blankets and dressed in much of her catering uniform still from last night. Only her apron was gone. I just hoped she knew where it was.

"Ash," I said in a stage whisper.

"Ashley's dead. Come back later," she whispered back.

"Did someone come over last night?" I asked.

"No." She twisted, looking up at me in confusion. "What do you mean?"

"Someone's in Mary's bed."

"It's Mary you dumb ass," Ash muttered, going back to her pillowed bliss.

"Yeah, Mary *and* someone else."

Ashley's face appeared again, confusion all over her features. "Who?"

"Can't tell."

"Oh man." She tried to push herself to her feet, but her body wouldn't cooperate. She collapsed back to the blankets with a whimper. "Can't check. You go." Her hand flapped at me. "Report back."

I was torn between a desire to crawl back into my bed and sleep for another four hours, and the intense need to know who was in Mary's bed. Curiosity won out, and I hobbled back into the hall and stood in my roommate's open doorway.

The shape beneath the blanket was larger and bulkier than Mary. A male shape for sure.

Here I had options: creep into the room and stare at them like a weirdo, waiting for the mystery man to reveal his face; cough awkwardly and hope they'd sense my presence; or take the bull by the horns and expose them. I went with the last option, grabbing the nearest edge of blanket and yanking it off of the two shapes.

It was Jake. Jake and Mary, snuggled in her bed like sleepy puppies. Mary was in an oversized University t-shirt, hitched up around her waist, exposing the Wonder Woman panties beneath. Jake in only his boxer shorts—and thank god for that—tucked in behind her with his arm draped over her bare waist.

They both made animal noises of protest, scrambling to grab hold of the bedding as I pulled it away from them.

"Hey!" Jake grunted.

Mary's eyes opened and went wide at the sight of me. "Emmy!" she protested.

"Em, come on, don't be a bitch," Jake said, leaning up on one elbow to make another reach for the blankets.

I tossed the covers onto them in a wad. "Just checking," I said, shambling back toward my own room.

A few seconds after I cleared Mary's doorway, the door banged shut behind me. I smiled to myself, still a bit too hung over to laugh.

"Who was it?" Ashley mumbled when I dropped onto my bed.

"Jake."

"Why am I not surprised?" she said. It really wasn't a surprise. Jake had clearly been crushing on Mary for about a year. And she didn't seem to mind a bit. I just hoped they'd both been clear-headed enough to enjoy themselves last night.

"She'll tell us later, I'm sure," I said, feeling much better now that I'd achieved a horizontal status again.

Ashley giggled suddenly. "I guess they got confused about who you were trying to get laid last night."

"Oh god, that actually happened?" I moaned.

"Oh yeah. You were real set on getting Beckett some rebound action."

"I was hoping I just imagined that."

"Nope."

"Ugh."

"Poor Beck," she said.

"Poor Beck," I agreed.

"I can hear you," came a gravelly voice from the hallway.

Ash and I both looked toward the door where Beckett was standing on wobbly legs.

"Oh shit!" Ashley said. "Are you part ninja or something?"

"Yes," he said immediately, then groaned and leaned against the doorway. "Or not."

"You okay?" I asked.

He looked surprisingly well put together all things consid-ered. I mean, hung over for sure. But he'd at least managed to get himself out of yesterday's clothes and into a pair of athletic shorts for sleeping. Or maybe he'd only done it after he got up. Either way, there was less walk of shame in him than the rest of us.

"Sure." His voice was thick with sleep and leftover alcohol. Without another word, he disappeared from view and a few minutes later, I heard the shower running in the guys' bathroom.

A while later—I wasn't sure how much time had passed—he was in the doorway again, tapping on the door lightly. We were generally pretty comfortable around each other as a group, but the guys tried to be respectful about coming into the girls' rooms without permission. Of course, all of that was kind of moot when Ash and I slept in our clothes with the door hanging wide open. Still, I appreciated it.

I raised my face from the pillow. "What's up?"

"You guys want some breakfast?"

"No!" Ashley moaned. I wondered if she was on a slightly different hangover timeline than me since she'd gotten started later than the rest of us.

I made a non-committal *mmph* sound.

"Come on, Em," he said.

I made another non-word sound.

"I'm buying."

That brought my eyes to full alert. Because the fact of the matter was that I was still broke and out of luck until Monday morning. Also, there was no way there was anything edible left in the house if we'd been eating mustard last night.

Ugh, mustard. The thought turned my stomach once again, but I fought it. "Okay. Gimme five minutes."

"I'll give you three," he said, before he walked away to give me some privacy.

I hauled myself out of bed and tipped the door shut before peeling off last night's clothes. Then I changed into some nice soft yoga pants and a tank top that didn't require a bra. Presentable, but not too challenging for my ravaged body. Then I stepped into my flip-flops and made my way downstairs.

Beckett was standing with his crossed arms propped on the kitchen counter and his head dropped on top of them like he was taking a nap. His light brown hair was still damp from the shower.

The kitchen was a disaster zone. Far worse than the last time I'd taken notice of it the night before.

"Holy crap," I sighed. "Did we have a bunch of lab monkeys on the loose in here last night?"

Now it was Beckett's turn to make a wordless grunting reply.

I spotted a half-empty bottle of water on one counter, tipped over, but with the cover on tight. My mouth cramped with thirst, but there was honestly no telling if that was even water at this point. There were empty liquor and beer bottles everywhere, food stains, a dish towel still soaking wet and dripping water into a healthy puddle off the edge of the counter. Pizza crumbs and a congealed bit of crust lying on the floor...it was horrifying.

"Let's get out of here," I suggested.

Beckett hauled himself upright and together we staggered out the front door into the bright glare of a California Saturday morning.

"Ow!" I yelped, splaying my fingers over my face. "I forgot my sunglasses."

"Fuck me." Beckett squinted hard at the ground.

"This is a bad idea."

He gestured back in the general direction of our apartment. "We've had a lot of bad ideas in the last 24 hours."

I groaned.

"Come on. We need food. Grease." Beckett took my elbow and gave me a push toward the sidewalk.

We walked in silence toward the main street at the end of the block. There was no way either of us was fit to drive. This was the purgatory between Still Drunk and Hung Over where you are both useless and no fun.

But it was a college town, after all, and we weren't the only dead drunks walking this morning. Out on the main drag, we joined the scattered collection of people staggering home in last night's clothes, as well as the rest of the people out trying to get their morning dose of hangover-healing grease in various collections of pajamas, and college spirit wear.

The line outside the nearest greasy spoon was out the door and down the block.

"No!" Beckett groaned.

"I can't wait that long," I told him.

"Me neither."

We continued down the street, passing shuttered bars, closed stores, a bike repair shop that seemed to be already open for business, and finally came to a Japanese tea house that Ashley and I had been to a few times for lunch. Miraculously the sign was turned to Open and there was a pleasant, salty smell coming from the place.

There was also no line.

"Here," I said.

"Do they even serve food in the morning?"

I pointed to the sign in the window that said 'Open for breakfast, Saturday & Sunday at 8am.'

Beckett shrugged. "All right, whatever."

We went inside, setting off a light tinkling of bells. There were some other customers inside, but most of them appeared to have their shit significantly more together than either of us. A young woman in a black t-shirt and skirt came over to greet us.

"Good morning," she said. "Would you like a table?"

We nodded and followed her to a small black cafe table near the window, which made me wish again that I'd grabbed my sunglasses.

"Tea?" she asked.

Beckett looked at me, as if to say, *Why the hell did you bring me to a land with no coffee?*

The waitress was holding out a small leather folder that was covered in a list of teas. Last time I'd been here, Ashley and I had poured over the list for a long time, trying to choose just one from the huge selection. Today, I couldn't be relied on to choose two matching socks from a field of three. I turned my pleading face to her and said, "We are very very hung over," in a soft voice. "What do you recommend?"

Her face brightened. "I've got just what you need!" She left without another word, or even leaving the menu behind.

"What the hell did you just do to us?" Beckett mumbled.

"I panicked!"

"I'm holding you responsible for whatever happens next."

"Fine. But just remember I'm broke, so you're paying for whatever happens next."

A fresh wave of awful seemed to take over him at that point and he put his head on upraised hands, breathing shallowly.

That was fine with me, I wasn't exactly in the mood for chatter. So we sat in rigid, but not uncomfortable silence while we both contemplated our life choices and the relative merits of throwing up versus fighting to keep everything in our stomachs exactly where it was.

When the waitress returned a few minutes later, she put a small bowl of clear miso soup in front of each of us, and then a pot of tea on a small ceramic ring to keep it from burning the table. Then she laid empty tea cups on the table.

"Soup first," she advised. "The tea will help, but some people don't like the taste very much."

That earned me a dirty look from Beckett, but he thanked her just the same.

When she was gone again, I took up my spoon and lifted a small sip of the steaming broth to my mouth. It was perfect. Not too salty, not too bland. It seemed to fit in my mouth as if it belonged there, and then greeted my stomach with a soothing presence, instead of the usual fight for dominance that my first bite of hangover food did.

I sighed happily. "Try it," I told Beckett. "Trust me."

He did, and I saw the same reaction bloom across his face. "Okay, so maybe this wasn't the worst plan you ever had."

We fell back into a companionable silence as we slurped our

magic elixir. My small bowl was empty in no time and I could have easily gone for seconds or thirds, but the waitress was nowhere to be seen.

"That was amazing," I said, feeling more human than I would have thought possible just minutes before. "I'm trying the tea."

The liquid from the teapot was yellow, with an earthy smell that didn't exactly soothe my palate the way the miso soup had. When I drank coffee, I was much more likely to go for something with caramel or -iatto in the name than anything in the bitter, dry-roasted, or black department. I rarely had tea without sugar and cream. But the waitress had been dead-on with her first offering, so I was willing to try it.

It tasted like dirt. Like a mouthful of garden soil. My stomach didn't threaten to revolt, exactly, but it did put out a Closed sign. Beckett was studying my reaction, though, and I didn't want to give anything away. So I forced myself to swallow.

There must have been something in my expression, though, because he said, "How is it?" in a skeptical tone.

"I usually like my tea sweetened," I said diplomatically, then shrugged. "I don't know. Try it."

He didn't pour himself a cup, but reached across the table to sample from mine.

The look on his face told me he was completely on the same page as me. "That is disgusting."

"Earthy," I supplied.

"I feel like I just licked the sidewalk." He stuck his tongue out, like exposing it to the air would evaporate the aftertaste.

"Maybe it's an acquired taste?" I wondered, reaching over to take my cup back and try another sip. Now that I knew what to expect, it wasn't such a shock, but the taste wasn't any better. "Maybe not?"

Beckett laughed then. A started bark of laughter that made his dimples show.

I couldn't help joining in. Not even sure why. But we were both gone at that point.

I managed to pour him a cup of his own dirt-flavored tea and told him he had to drink it. We were still bickering about it when the waitress returned with a tray in her arms.

"You don't like the tea?" she asked, maintaining an impressive poker face.

"It's...different," I said.

"Turmeric," she said. "You get used to it. Very good for the liver."

"God knows my liver could use a jump start this morning," Beckett said, taking another huge gulp of tea. His face curled into a hideous grimace, but he swallowed and said, "Mmm. Yum."

The waitress laughed and set two more small bowls in front of us before clearing our empty soup cups. The fresh bowls were filled with rice, which I recognized immediately. But I also recognized the raw egg settled into a small depression in the rice.

"Tamago kake gohan," she announced. "You have to stir it for a long time." She set down two pairs of chop sticks and a bottle of soy sauce as well as a shaker of some kind of seasoning. "Stir, stir, stir, and add these to your liking."

When she was gone, Beckett said, "Fuck it," and set to work blending the egg into his rice, humming the Rocky theme song.

After making him drink the tea, I could hardly let him show me up with the main course, so I followed suit, whirling my chop sticks through the bowl until the egg turned frothy. Beckett beat me to it, though, hoisting a bite into his mouth. He made a face, then added a bunch of soy sauce to the mix. Another taste, and he shook some of the seasoning blend on top. Finally he nodded with satisfaction.

"Try it," he said. "It's not bad."

I was completely aware of the possibility that he was getting back at me for the turmeric tea, but I had a feeling he was sincere. So I copied his technique and took a tentative bite.

He was right. It wasn't bad. In fact it was kind of good. Comforting and simple, like the miso had been.

Yet another silence settled over us as we dove into our unusual hangover feast. Even the turmeric tea seemed less pungent as I took a few more sips between bites. Was I magically cured of all hangover symptoms? No. My head was still aching and I had the bone deep fatigue of bad decisions hanging over me, but my stomach had settled considerably and I felt less foggy. A lot further from death.

When we were finished, Beckett laid his chopsticks across his empty bowl and regarded me. "Okay, fine. So, it wasn't a bad choice."

"You can say it: Emmy is a golden goddess."

"Yeah, that's exactly what I was thinking."

"I'll accept, Emmy makes better life choices than Beckett," I continued.

"Except for roommate hunting on Craigslist," he pointed out.

"Now that's just mean."

"Sorry," he said, but he grinned.

I sighed and propped my chin on one hand. "Ugh. I guess I know how I'm spending my day. Apartment hunting online." With only days left in my current living situation, the clock was ticking. Moving to a new city was intimidating enough without the added stress of having no place to put my stuff when I got there.

Beckett and I had that in common at least. We were both going to the tiny town of River Glen, Iowa for grad school. Maybe it seemed unlikely that we'd end up at the same small school, but Beck and I had met as biology majors as freshmen. I'd wanted to work in a lab ever since my first frog dissection in middle school. Beckett had considered medical school, but ultimately decided to be a pathologist's assistant just like me. All the dissecting goodness without the years and debt of being a doctor. And with only a dozen graduate programs in the country, it wasn't that weird that we'd both landed at a tiny private school in Iowa. We counted ourselves lucky to have both gotten into the program. And it was way easier to contemplate moving to a new state with someone I knew. Sure, Beckett was supposed to get married and live with Emily when we got there, but that didn't mean we couldn't stay friends.

It was part of the reason I'd gone into the stupid Craigslist agreement in the first place: I wasn't looking for a best friend in my roommate, just a clean place to live close to campus. I thought it might be better to have more of a business arrangement. I mean, there was no way I could expect to fall into another amazing group of friends who were more like family, as I'd done in undergrad. And I didn't want to. I wanted them to stay important in my life. So a stranger looking for a roommate seemed like a perfectly acceptable solution.

Besides, the pics of the place had been great—light, airy, with two bathrooms. Two!

I guess I should have known that was too good to be true. What kind of campus-accessible apartment has a bathroom for each bedroom?

God, I'm an idiot sometimes.

Apartment hunting remotely was awful. There is just no substitute for going into a place and seeing it for yourself. Pictures can be deceiving. And, as it turns out, so can the people who put the pictures up.

I shook my head ruefully. I couldn't believe I'd been duped like that. Maybe I could find a nice Nigerian Prince who just needed a loan to get back his family fortune next. Ugh.

"Don't stress, Em. I'm sure there are still places to live," Beckett said as if he could read my thoughts.

"I hope you're right."

"There better be," he said with a sigh of his own. "Because I sure as hell don't qualify for my place without Emily."

Married Student Housing. It was such a foreign concept to

31

me. I knew there were apartment blocks right here on campus for couples, especially those with kids. But I didn't know where the heck they were or who lived there.

The culture at Middlesex University was totally different than here, though. Everyone in the undergrad program was required to live on campus. Grad students had more leeway, thought they were encouraged to live on campus as well. And it wasn't like there was a huge glut of student-friendly housing near campus. It wasn't a college town like Irvine. The entire city didn't revolve around the comings and goings of students.

"Maybe we could find a place together!" I suggested with sudden inspiration.

"Yeah?"

"Sure!" I nodded enthusiastically. "It would be so much better than having to find a place that needed a roommate."

"Yeah." The idea was working for him, I could see it. "Yeah, duh. Of course. Why didn't I think of it right away?"

"Vodka," I answered.

He laughed. "Yeah, maybe."

"But this is perfect! We're great at being roommates! It'll be like nothing's changed."

"We'll probably have to share a bathroom," he warned me.

I wrinkled my nose. "You'll just have to learn how to live like a human being instead of a goat."

"It's mostly Brady, you know," he said.

I could sort of believe that, but I wasn't letting him off the hook that easily. "I'm sure there's room for improvement. But still, it's a deal?" I held my hand out to him across the remnants of our breakfast.

"Hell yeah, it's a deal."

We shook on it.

4

REALITY BITES. AND SO DOES REALTY.

A deal was one thing. The ability to make it come to life turned out to be a totally different idea.

The real estate listings in River Glen were slim pickings. There wasn't much available at all, especially when you factored in our lack of transportation. Beckett had a car, but I didn't. Which ruled out any major distances from campus. And considering it was an old, gated institution with a long winding walk from the nearest parking area, that really cut down on what we could realistically look at.

It seemed like the listings were aimed in two distinct directions: whole house rentals for professors with families that were so far out of our price range it was laughable, and single rooms for rent in boarding houses. Of which there were two. One had a shared bathroom and was only available until mid-October. The other was for women only and included the caveat that there were multiple cats on the property. No one with allergies need apply.

That meant me.

"What are we going to do?" I asked Beckett, throwing up my hands in resignation.

He shook his head. "Maybe they've got one of those room-mate matching sites for grad students..." he muttered, clicking through screen after screen on the Student Services website.

"Maybe it would have been helpful if we'd had more than a few days' notice to start this search." Collapsing back on the couch, I muttered, "Fucking Craigslist. Fucking Emily."

Beckett only sighed.

"Besides, this entire thing is going to be pointless if I can't get my money back. I can't even pay tuition for the fall!" I covered my face with my hands. "Maybe I should just defer. Stay here and get a job for now. You know there are always people looking for roommates around here."

One thing was for sure, I couldn't go home. I didn't really have a home these days. Ever since my mom died, my dad had been living out his dream of driving cross-country on his Harley. He'd sold our house in San Jose. Sold everything. He'd probably welcome me joining him on the road, but that was not the life I was looking for. Sitting bitch or hunkered down in a sidecar? No thanks.

I hadn't even had the courage to call my dad yet and tell him about getting all my money stolen. I didn't think he'd blame me or anything, but the reality was, there wasn't a whole lot he could do for me, except tell me how sorry he was. He'd probably have a little bit of money he could give me to tide me over, and it might come to that if the bank said I was screwed, but I hated to ask.

Beckett turned slowly to look at me. "Wait—you're Emily."

"Yeah. Hi. We've met." No one called me Emily anyway. I was always Emmy, or Em.

"You're Emily," he repeated. "Like Emily."

It wasn't like it was an unusual name. Hell, you could throw a rock and hit a girl named Emily around campus. I couldn't see his point. "Beck, what are you talking about?"

"I *have* a place to live," he said. "With Emily. You could be Emily. You *are* Emily."

"What?"

"I've still got a place. *On* campus. All I need to keep it is an Emily. And you happen to be an Emily."

I shook my head. "That would never work. Don't they know her name? Her *real* name, I mean? Emily Wilson? They must know she decided not to come to school there. They've got to cancel her housing, too, don't they?"

"Let me check something..." He set back to work on the computer, tapping his way through screens until he found what he was looking for. "Married student housing is available to students with dependents, with preference given to those families with children," he read aloud. "Just because Emily withdrew from the university doesn't mean she couldn't live with me."

"Beck, that's crazy. We'd never get away with it."

He opened his mouth like he wanted to protest, but nothing came out. His shoulders drooped. "You're probably right."

"We'll just—" I spread my hands out in a calming gesture. "We'll figure something out."

∾

THE BANK WAS both good news and bad news. The good news was that they were willing to believe that I hadn't authorized the three checks that Bonnie had written out of my account, effectively bankrupting me. The bad news was, it was going to take some time to go through their fraud review process and get me back my money.

I lost several hours of my life in the bank branch, changing my account numbers, filling out forms, and getting new cards issued on everything. There were calls to the police who had taken my statement, and affidavits to be obtained.

In the end, I wasn't going to lose any more money—which would have been pretty hard anyway, considering my balance was negative $1,739.58—and eventually I'd have all my lost funds returned. But it would be at least six weeks. And considering I'd given notice at my lab job, there wasn't going to be any money coming in any time soon.

There was no way I could avoid getting my father involved.

Damn it. I was not good at admitting I needed help.

I decided to head home and focus on packing. Because when your life is full of question marks, sometimes it's just easier to sink your teeth into something that you can completely control. And no matter what else happened, at the end of the week I was going to move out of the apartment I'd called home for two years. Nothing would slow that change. I'd just have to roll with it.

Ashley had the same idea, apparently, because I found her folding clothes into a black garbage bag on the floor between our beds.

"Hey sweetie, how'd it go?" she asked when I tossed my stuff on the bed.

"Okay, I guess." I told her the story of the bank.

"There's nothing else they can do?"

"Nope."

"Didn't you give them some of this?" She pouted her lips and opened her eyes cartoonishly wide in imitation of me. "Nobody can resist your big green peepers, don't they know that?"

I laughed. "Apparently not."

"So you're stuck with that negative balance for six weeks?" she demanded.

"No, they brought me back up to zero and then they credited my paycheck from yesterday." Depositing my last check was how I found out about the whole fiasco in the first place. I'd fed the check into a nearby ATM for deposit and was horrified to see the four-digit number in red on the receipt.

"Oh, well, that's better than nothing, anyway."

"Better than less than nothing, you mean."

"Seriously."

"I can't believe we're not going to be roommates anymore." She made a sad face, but it wasn't supposed to be an impression of me this time.

"I know."

Letting the sweater in her hands drop to the bed, she closed the space between us and gave me a quick hug. "God, I'm going to miss everyone so much!"

"I know, me too." My eyes stung with tears, but I didn't want to get started down that path again. So I took a cleansing breath and refocused. "Got another one of those bags?"

"You bet."

Ash and I worked together for a while, chatting about nothing, deciding who would get to keep certain items we'd accumulated together over the years. Nothing major—a DVD copy of *Pitch Perfect*, or the sign that hung on the door of our freshman year dorm room: *Ashley and ~~Emily~~ Emmy*. It had hung on every door that we'd had for four years. Eventually we decided we'd each keep a picture of it on our phones and leave it taped to the back of the closet so the next occupants of our room would know whose territory they were taking over.

"Are you and Beckett still driving to Iowa together on Friday?"

Of all the things we'd talked about, Beckett and I hadn't addressed how our travel plans might change. Obviously, it made sense that we were going to drive to River Glen together from here. But we'd originally planned a stop in Phoenix. My dad was going to meet me there and we'd have the weekend together while Beckett and Emily did their quickie wedding.

Thinking about it now, it seemed utterly unromantic and robotic. Like getting married was just an item on a checklist instead of a lifelong commitment. I couldn't help being glad that he wasn't going through with it.

"I'm really not sure. Neither of us has anywhere to go until August 23rd. I'm literally homeless."

"Come home with me!" Ashley suggested. "You both can! It'll be so fun!"

"My dad…" I hedged, but going to Ashley's place in Nevada sounded like a lot more fun than hanging around in Phoenix for no reason.

"Come on! Let's tell Beckett. You guys could use a little fun." She grinned at me. "Plus…it's a free place to stay and my mom will cook so much food you'll probably get fat by the end of the week."

It sounded good. It sounded like more of a plan than I'd had since I saw that damn ATM receipt.

"Maybe that would work…" I chewed my lip, wondering how mad my dad would be if I changed our plans.

"It's a great idea!" Ashley waggled her eyebrows suggestively, then rushed out of the room shouting, "Beckett!"

Which is how I ended up sitting poolside with a margarita in a cactus-stemmed glass in Henderson, Nevada just a week after losing everything I had.

Life is very weird sometimes.

~

ASHLEY HAD BEEN RIGHT, her parents were thrilled to have all of us stay with them. They had plenty of room—including an empty stall in their four-car garage where they let us pile all the stuff we'd had to strap to the roof of Beckett's RAV4. We'd lived in a furnished apartment for two years, but somehow we'd still managed to accumulate more crap than we could possibly fit in the trunk and backseat of his compact SUV.

The change in scenery didn't come with solutions to our housing problem, unfortunately, but at least it was more comfortable to be screwed when you had a beautiful in-ground pool to soak away your troubles in.

My dad had been understanding. In fact, he was in Utah when

I'd reached him, so he decided to swing through Nevada instead of beelining it to Arizona after all. He said he'd rather see Reno than Phoenix anyway. Not Las Vegas. Reno. My dad was such a weirdo sometimes.

The water droplets glinting off Ashley's wet body as she emerged from the pool sent fractals of light into my eyes, and I guarded the top of my sunglasses with one hand. After a summer of working her ass off in dark catering halls, Ashley was soaking up sun like a hungry house plant. Her black hair was streaked with reddish highlights and her skin was deeply tanned. She squeezed the water out of her hair and settled next to me on a matching lounge chair.

"He's still talking, huh?" she asked, nodding toward the far end of the deck where Beckett was standing with his phone pressed to his ear in a tiny patch of shade afforded by the setting sun.

"Yeah. It's the first time she's actually spoken to him since the email."

"I hate to say it, but what a bitch."

Emily had called Beckett out of the blue nearly an hour ago. Maybe it was the fact that tomorrow was originally supposed to be the day they got married? Maybe she was having second-second thoughts? I didn't know, and he'd been staying out of earshot for the entire conversation, so we'd just have to wait.

His margarita was nothing but a cup of warm pink liquid in the bottom of his abandoned glass.

Behind us, Ashley's dad was manning a grill full of kebabs, while her mom was still in the kitchen finishing up some side dishes.

Finally, we saw Beckett lower the phone from his ear and take a last, long glance at the screen before tucking it into the pocket of his swim trunks. He didn't leave his secluded shady spot for a few more minutes, though, instead staring across the fence to the desert just beyond Ash's neighborhood.

When he came toward us, I felt a moment of panic. Were we supposed to act like nothing had happened? Should we ask right away? I shot a glance at Ashley and thought I detected the same note of uncertainty in her eyes.

Beckett solved the quandary for us though, saying, "Well, that's that," as soon as he was within earshot.

"What happened?" Ashley asked.

"Honestly? Not a whole lot."

"Seemed like it took a long time for not a whole lot," I said.

"Yeah," he agreed, dropping to sit on the lounger to my right. He picked up his forgotten margarita glass and swirled the liquid in it dubiously before putting it back on the ground. "Basically, she just doesn't think this is the right decision."

Ashley sucked air through her teeth. "I mean…is she wrong?"

"I guess not," Beckett retrieved the sunglasses he'd left on the end of his chair and put them on, hiding his expression a bit. "I just wish she'd said something earlier."

"Maybe she didn't know?" I suggested, trying to give him a bit of hope.

He lowered his glasses to look at me for a moment. "She re-enrolled at Arizona in the spring."

"Oh."

"Yeah. Covering all her bases I guess."

"Sorry," I said.

He exhaled. "Whatever. I don't want to talk about it, okay?"

Ash and I exchanged glances, but agreed.

5

WHAT COULD GO WRONG?

*L*ate that night, I found myself awake for no reason, so I decided to get myself a glass of water. Leaving the room that had once belonged to Ashley's sister Karma, I padded down to the cool stone hallway to the kitchen.

Through the big sliding doors, I spotted a human form on the pool deck and adrenaline jolted me. Intruder?

I froze in the dark kitchen, barely daring to breathe, until I saw the shape move. It was just too familiar. Beckett.

He hadn't been sleeping well, I knew, and I couldn't really blame him. Maybe he would have preferred to be alone, but I couldn't leave him without at least checking. So I let myself out onto the deck.

The heat of the day had been vacuumed up by the shocking cool of the desert night and I found myself shivering in surprise. My sleep clothes of shorts and a t-shirt didn't feel like enough. But then I realized that Beckett was sitting on the edge of the hot tub with his feet dangling in the hot water. Smart boy.

Huddling my arms around my chest, I approached him. "Hey, is there room for two here?"

He looked up in surprise. "What are you doing up?"

I shrugged. "Just thirsty. I saw you through the window. Is that okay?"

"Pull up a slab of concrete." He patted the ground next to him.

Settling beside him, I let my feet sink into the steamy water with a hiss. "Ooh, that's hot."

"Give it a second."

I did, gazing up at the dark sky and all the scattered stars across it. There was light pollution on the horizon, but the display was still impressive here. Much more than we'd had back in Irvine. "Wow."

"I know, right?" He leaned back on his hands, tilting his face up. "I wish I knew more about what I was looking at."

I pointed. "That's Cassiopeia. And that's the Dragon. And that one's called the Church."

"Really?"

"I don't know."

He laughed, and nudged me with his elbow. "Is the Church even a real constellation?"

"If it's not, it should be." I said.

"I guess you'll just have to discover a star and you can name it whatever you want."

"I'd have to discover a whole constellation, wouldn't I?"

"If you want to be picky about it."

We fell silent, staring into the void. As always, the longer I looked at the areas I thought were dark, the more tiny pinpricks of light revealed themselves.

"Do you think the entire sky is actually stars?"

"What?"

"You know how they keep finding stars in all the dark spaces? Those deep space telescopes and all that?"

"Oh yeah."

"I wonder if we could actually see them all—" I raised my hands above us and made a squishing gesture. "Like compress all of space into something two dimensional, would the entire thing be so filled with stars that there would be no black parts?"

"I don't know," he said wonderingly. "I guess it's possible."

"It would be bright all the time."

"But you wouldn't actually be able to see them. They'd all blur together."

"That's true."

We stared long enough that I caught three shooting stars. Then I nudged him with my shoulder. "You doing okay?"

"Good enough."

"Really?"

"Well what the hell else am I going to say? I feel...gutted. Like I don't even know what's real anymore." He sighed. "I hate the phrase, 'turned the world upside down' but seriously that's how I feel."

"Nothing she said today helped, huh?"

"She said she still loves me." He snorted. "Like, hoo-fucking-ray, I'm going to ruin your life, but it's okay because I still love you."

"Do you think—" I paused, not sure if this was a question I could honestly expect him to answer. "Are you, like, staying together?"

"No." But he didn't sound completely sure. "I mean, she called off the wedding. She secretly dropped out of the school we were supposed to go to together. And she wouldn't even talk to me for almost a week. What part of that says, 'Stay with me!'?"

"I see your point."

"But clearly, I don't know anything about anything, so hey, maybe I'm wrong."

I found his hand, clutching it tightly in both of mine. "This isn't your fault."

"Yeah, maybe. But it feels awfully personal."

"You didn't do anything wrong. You did everything she and

her crazy parents wanted. I mean, seriously, Beck, you did way more than the average guy would do."

"It's like she doesn't even care that this is seriously ruining my life." His voice cracked and he muttered, "Fuck. She doesn't even care that I still have to deal with her mess."

"She and Bonnie have that in common."

"Who?" He turned to me in confusion. "Oh right. Yeah, I guess they do, don't they?"

With nothing new to say on that front, I just gave his hand a squeeze and stayed quiet.

The hot tub began some automatic cycle around us, an unseen motor humming softly and a light fizz of bubbles tickling our legs.

"Emily said when she pulled out of Middlesex, she made sure to tell them that I was still going. That I'd still need housing."

"Well, that was...thoughtful?"

"Go figure that, huh?" He continued. "I know I should contact the housing department and tell them what happened. I know I'm going to end up screwed on this. But we're already moving to fucking River Glen, why would I voluntarily give up the one place I actually know I can live? Why should Emily be able to take that from me?"

The bubble of avoidance here at Ashley's house was thin, but I had clung to it for days. I still had no idea what I was going to do when we got to Middlesex. Throw myself on the mercy of the housing department? End up sleeping in a bus station? Camp in the middle of the quad? I had less than zero ideas.

"I'll be your Emily," I announced, almost before I knew I was going to speak.

"You will?" He knew immediately what I meant.

"What the hell else are we going to do? I am literally homeless, Beck. Seriously, what options do I have?" I looked at him. "You have a home but no Emily. I am an Emily and I have no home. I mean, what are the odds?"

44

He smiled. "Pretty small, I guess."

"So...okay. We'll go, we'll move into your place. In six weeks, I should have all my money back. That should be plenty of time to find another place to live, right? Someone is bound to fail out by then and have to move out."

"That's the spirit!" He grinned. "Hope for others' failure!"

"This is what my life has become," I said.

"So, we're doing this?" he asked. "We're scamming the system?"

"Yes."

"You'll be my Emily?"

"Just promise you'll keep calling me Emmy."

"Promise."

"Then, we're roommates." I said. "Again."

"Roommates," he agreed. "You are a life saver."

"You're the life saver," I said. "Remember? Literally homeless."

"We both would have been, Em."

"Well, not anymore. Now we're...fake platonic husband and wife...until we get caught."

"We won't get caught."

6

GOING TO THE CHAPEL

*W*e didn't tell anyone what we'd decided. It was time for Beckett and me to be on our way to River Glen anyway, and it didn't take much deep soul searching to figure out that Ashley might think this was a stupid plan. Mostly because it was a stupid plan, I guess. But when your back is against the wall, any lifeline will do. Or some other metaphor that makes sense.

So with our terrible plan in hand, Beckett and I packed up his RAV4 and hit the road, next stop Las Vegas. Because there was one more little detail in agreeing to be his Emily: turns out that the housing authority at Middlesex would be asking to see our marriage license.

Beckett and I were going to get married.

As we rolled into the city limits, past that famous 1960s era *Welcome* sign, butterflies began to flutter in my stomach. I was going to get married.

Married.

We'd talked it through on the drive, and we'd agreed that as soon as we got our living arrangements settled, we'd get an annulment. That way we'd never even have to tell anyone about it. It would be like it had never happened at all. A legal contract, nothing more. We'd be like business partners. It wasn't about love, romance, or even our friendship. It was a really, really formal roommate agreement.

Those were the thoughts that ran through my head like a litany as we followed the GPS directions to the Regional Justice Center. Beckett found a place to park and we went inside to get our place in line. It was just after eight in the morning on a weekday, so there wasn't much of a wait. Most people weren't drunk enough to make this kind of mistake yet, I guess.

All we had to do was show our drivers' licenses to get the marriage license. It was disturbingly easy. Then, in what is probably the classiest moment of my life, we asked where the quickest, cheapest place to get married was. The bored bureaucrat behind the counter pointed us to a nearby chapel offering something called The Sign & Go. Ah, romance.

On our way, we passed the famous chapel that offered Drive-Thru weddings. Talk about a marriage of convenience. This was obviously the right city for people like us.

At the chapel, the woman behind the check-in desk gave us a binder with different wedding packages. They ranged from the most basic to some truly over-the-top variations, including having an Elvis impersonator as our officiant. There were add-ons, too. Like a commemorative photo package, a bouquet that I could keep, and even a selection of rental wedding gowns.

"This will be fine," I told the woman, pinching the side seam of my sundress. It was just a typical dress that I'd worn dozens of times, bright red with white polka dots. Definitely not a wedding dress. But I couldn't stomach the idea of the big poufy princess gown for this sham marriage. Especially not one worn by a bunch of other women.

"Which package are you going with?" she asked with a big, Vegas-style smile. Her tanned face looked like it was slowly turning to leather below her tall blond hair.

"Just the Sign and Go, please," Beckett said, flipping the laminated pages back to the beginning.

The leathery woman's penciled-in eyebrows went up. "You don't want to make it a little more special?"

We looked at each other, then back at her. "No, thanks. Just need to get married."

"Suit yourself," she said in resignation.

Beckett gave her a tight smile. "Thanks."

We accepted a black buzzer like you get at a restaurant and took a seat on a round couch in the center of the waiting room. The other couple waiting for their turn was on a small love seat by the chapel doors, holding hands and gazing at each other as if blinking might make the other disappear. Over and over again they leaned close to kiss each other, not all of them PG.

I kept my hands in my lap, sitting near Beckett but not close enough to touch him. There were a million things I wanted to say, but none of them seemed right.

Today was his wedding day. The actual day he was supposed to marry his Emily. He was supposed to be in Arizona right now, probably dressed in a suit and waiting anxiously with his best man—his brother. Waiting with his high school sweetheart to begin the rest of his life.

Instead he was in a second-rate Vegas chapel with his roommate, wearing khaki shorts and a dark blue t-shirt.

I'm sorry I'm not Emily, I thought. *I'm sorry this is happening. I'm sorry you have to pay for it because I'm broke. Thank you for saving me. Thanks for putting your broken heart on hold so I have a place to live.*

Instead I glanced at him and said, "Okay?" in a low voice.

He nodded. "You?"

"Yep. I'm good." Sort of.

I caught the woman behind the desk looking at us suspiciously. She saw me catch her in the act and frowned deliberately.

I smiled at her and scooted a bit closer to Beckett. He startled out of his thoughts and gave me a confused look.

"I don't think we look like two people about to get married," I whispered.

He looked over at the desk woman, at the other couple in the waiting area, then back at me. "Right." He took my hand out of my lap, weaving our fingers together letting our hands rest on his thigh. The act made my heart jitter with guilty nerves. Like the woman would somehow see through us and intuit that we were attempting to scam the housing department of a small university in Iowa.

"Why does she even care?" I whispered. "I'm sure there are plenty of people who get married for dumber reasons than this."

Beckett grinned. "She's a romantic at heart, I guess."

I laughed. "Yeah, that's definitely it."

I'd never held hands with him like this and I was surprised that he kept stroking his thumb over mine. It was sweet, and probably an unconscious bit of muscle memory from Emily.

The chapel doors opened and another couple emerged, holding their arms aloft in victory, smiling and laughing and pursued by an employee with white confetti. The couple, who were both men in their fifties, threw their arms around each other and kissed while "Trumpet Voluntary" played from somewhere inside the chapel.

After a moment, the officiant, who was a big, sweaty-faced man in a purple robe that looked like it might have once been worn by a Gospel choir member, followed them out. "Who's my nine-fifteen?" he asked.

The kissy couple by the doors hopped up, the woman shouting, "We are!" She was in her twenties, I'd guess, not too much older than we were, while her groom appeared to be at least 15 years older than that. Maybe more.

"That relationship has long-term written all over it," Beckett observed drily.

The two buoyant men who'd just gotten hitched walked past us, their arms entwined and their faces lit up like Christmas trees.

"Congratulations," I said when one of them made eye contact with me.

"Thank you!" he said excitedly.

Then they disappeared into a side room to get some pictures taken, and Beck and I were alone in the waiting room with the Queen of Judgement. We sat in silence for a few minutes, holding hands.

"Still okay?" I finally whispered.

"Yep."

That was all either of us said until the May-to-December couple emerged a few minutes later, practically tripping over each other as they tried to walk and suck face at the same time. Once again the officiant followed them out and looked around the waiting area.

"You must be my nine-thirty," he said.

"That's us," Beckett agreed, standing without letting go of my hand. I popped up awkwardly beside him.

"You ready to get married?" the purple-robed man asked.

"Yep."

"Let's do this."

We followed him into the chapel room, which was not much larger than a decent-sized bedroom. There were chairs arranged in two squads on either side of an aisle, but no more than 16 on each side, and they looked like they spent at least ninety percent of every day completely unoccupied. The chairs in the last rows had dust on the upholstery. Opposite the doors, a black velvet curtain hung the length of the room with a small table centered in front of it and two large flower arrangements that reminded me of a funeral home more than a wedding. Off to the side, an organ was angled toward the "altar" with a woman seated on a bench behind it. There were two other employees in the room; a man sitting in the front row, looking bored, and a woman standing at a high top table just inside the door.

"Here we go, bride," she said, approaching me with something white in her hands. It floofed in the air and then I had a headband plunked on my head. The attached tulle fell forward around my shoulders, standing out stiffly like a triangle. Then the woman held out a small bouquet of fake roses, all white and pink with plenty of baby's breath and white lace surrounding it.

"No, no," I protested. "We just wanted the Sign and Go thing."

"Yeah, we paid for the basic thing," Beckett agreed.

The woman wrinkled her nose. "Nobody wants that."

"No, seriously," I said, trying to detangle the veil from my hair.

"We've got a few extra minutes," the officiant said. "Why not go for something a little more special?"

"We already paid," Beckett said.

"You've already got the veil on," the woman by the door added. "Come on, live a little."

"But we didn't pay for this," I tried.

"Tell you what, it's on the house," the officiant said. "Let's just get a move on, okay?" He consulted a paper in his hand, "Beckett, is it? You come with me."

Beckett looked at me questioningly. I shrugged, panic making my eyes wide like dinner plates.

"If you'll come with me," the officiant repeated, sounding mildly annoyed now. So Beckett followed him up to the altar.

"What do I do?" I asked the bouquet woman.

"Wait for the music, honey."

It wasn't a long wait. I barely had time to experience the swell of nausea in my gut before the organist began to play the "Wedding March" and the bouquet woman gave me a pat on the back.

"Down you go, honey."

"What?"

"That way." She pointed to the front of the room. "Get married, remember?"

I hurried down the aisle to stand beside Beckett, rushing through less than a single chorus of the "Wedding March," but that didn't seem to deter the organist. She made us stand there while she played through enough measures to satisfy some internal set point, then cut off abruptly.

The officiant began, "We are gathered here today to witness the marriage of..." he paused to look at the paper again, "Beckett Anderson and Emily Black."

The rest continued at a breakneck pace, with both of us promising that we were here of our own free will and—shocking —no one in the room objecting. We each repeated the short vows after the officiant, though I felt like I was listening to someone else use my lips and breath to form the words. My brain was churning and grasping for reality while the words came out of my mouth on autopilot. I couldn't have repeated them even a second later.

And then I heard the big purple man say, "By the power vested in me by the great state of Nevada, I know pronounce you husband and wife. You may kiss the bride."

Beckett looked at me with shock. The same shock that rattled through me. Kiss the bride? How had neither of us thought of that?

Before I could wrap my head around it, Beckett was leaning toward me and I felt the swift press of his lips on mine.

And then it was over. The organist began to play again and the officiant gestured for us to make our way down the aisle. Beckett took my hand and we walked away to the spray of white confetti from the two witnesses.

The last stop was in the lobby to sign our names on the marriage certificate along with our two "witnesses."

"Don't forget to sign your new name," the leathery blond told me, but I signed it "Emily Black." She did her eyebrow lift again, but didn't comment. I handed over the headband veil and my bouquet, we said no to the photographs she offered for a second time, and then we were on our way.

We were married.

7

A NIGHT TO FORGET

e finally called it quits on our drive for the night near Grand Junction, Colorado. It was getting dark and Beckett didn't want to drive through the mountains after sundown. My father had given me hotel gift cards to help cover my expenses while I waited for my fraud case to clear, so we drove until we found one in the right chain and asked for a room.

The room was small, and we filled up what limited floor space we had with our most precious possessions from the car. The things we absolutely could not afford to have stolen. Then we took turns in the bathroom, showering and getting into pajamas before climbing into the two double beds. It was the first time we'd slept in the same room together, but surrounded by so much of our junk, and exhausted after a long day on the road, it didn't feel weird. Plus, we each had our own bed, and we'd seen each other in pajamas hundreds of times while we were roommates.

Beckett turned off the TV when I finished in the bathroom. I crawled under the sheets in my bed. He pushed himself up on his elbow and reached for the switch on the nearby lamp, but before he turned it off he looked at me.

"So, is it what you always imagined your wedding night would be?" he asked.

I giggled. "Yes. Exactly like this."

"Me, too." He leaned out into the void between our beds, extending one hand as far as possible for a high five. I squirmed to the edge of the bed and gave his palm a slap before settling onto my side, facing him.

"Thank you for saving me," I said.

"Saving you?" he echoed. "From what?"

"Homelessness."

"You're the one saving me," he said.

I just looked at him.

"Let's say we saved each other and be done with it, okay?"

"Okay."

Beckett snapped off the lamp, though a crack in the curtains left a thin streak of light across both of our beds. "If we get going early tomorrow, we should make it all the way to River Glen."

"It's fifteen hours. Even if we make it there, it'll be so late, we won't be able to get into the apartment."

"We'll get as far as we can."

"Okay."

There was a silence so long I assumed he'd fallen asleep when he spoke again. "Who do you think is having a better wedding night? The gay guys or the face sucking couple?"

"I like to think the gay guys."

"Why's that?"

"I bet the other couple already used up his six hours of Viagra and he's passed out by now."

Beckett laughed. "All right, but that sounds like they had an awfully good wedding day."

"If that's what you're into."

"Six hours of sex and a good night's sleep? Sounds pretty good to me."

"Sounds like a recipe for chafing to me."

He hummed in a considering way. "Okay maybe not six *full* hours."

"Actually, I change my answer."

"To what?"

"I bet the organ player and the big purple officiant are having the best night of all."

Now he burst out laughing. "You're so right."

Smiling to myself, I rolled onto my other side, away from him. "Get some sleep, Beck."

"Good night, Mrs. Anderson."

"I kept my name, Mr. Black," I corrected, calling him by my last name just to irk him.

"Oh, right. Good night, Emmy."

～

THE ALARM CAME, as all alarms do, way too early. I groaned and slapped around on the nightstand until I found my phone, squinting at the screen to kill the buzzing and chirping. Only seconds later, Beckett's alarm started up on his phone, so I buried my head under the pillow. He silenced it, but I didn't move.

"Em," he said. "Em."

I didn't answer.

"Emmy. Time to get up."

A moment later, the first pillow landed on me, then another. When I didn't respond, he got up and picked up one of the tossed pillows to start hitting me with it.

"All right, all right!" I hollered after the barrage continued for uncounted minutes. When I unburied my head, my hair plastered all over my face, he was looming over me looking sleepy, but amused.

"Up and at 'em."

"Coffee."

"Absolutely," he agreed, so I swung my legs off the side and sat up. Then he added, "After we reload the car."

We played luggage Tetris for a few minutes until everything was back in the RAV4, then we hit the road in search of Starbucks. Thankfully it was only a mile down the road until we found one, and then we were on our way.

Beckett took the first shift of driving as we made our way through the high passes of the Rocky Mountains. The views were truly breathtaking, and more than once we pulled over to a scenic overlook to gape at the snowy peaks in the distance and take pictures. I sent a few selfies off to Ashley and Mary to show them we were making good time.

Once we were past Denver, Beckett let me have a turn behind the wheel, while he played DJ. The tunes ranged from current songs to the dawn of rock n' roll in the 1950s and we sang along at the top of our lungs. In the long stretch of I-80 that lead to Lincoln Nebraska, we got so bored with the straight line of pavement that we decided to see if we could remember every line of dialogue from the movie Elf, which had been Brady's favorite movie. And not just at Christmas time. Brady watched it multiple times a year. Probably multiple times a month. It was the most annoying and endearing thing about him.

At a rest stop near the exit for the amazingly named McCool Junction, Nebraska, I refused to get back in the car for an extra ten minutes.

"We have to walk," I told him solemnly. "Or we're not going to survive this trip."

"I don't think we'll actually die of sitting still."

"No, but I may commit murder-suicide if I don't get to stretch my legs a little."

"Well, I definitely don't want you going to jail in Nebraska," he said. "No one would ever come to visit you."

"Not even you?" I asked.

"Emmy, you literally just said you were going to kill me."

"Oh, right."

"My wife, ladies and gentlemen," he said, doing a ta-da gesture toward me.

"Ha ha. Shut up and walk with me." I led him along the entire length of the parking lot, past all the road dusty cars, and the RVs with far-flung license plates. Past the humming row of semi-trailers in the far part of the lot. Along the Pet Exercise area, where there were currently no animals exercising.

"Why don't they just say dogs?" Beckett wondered. "I mean, what other kind of pet would someone need to exercise here?"

"Gecko," I said immediately.

"Snakes, too?" he asked.

"God, I hope not."

"You're probably right. They just get their exercise slithering around the car."

I shuddered. "Ugh. Now I'm going to have nightmares."

"Just sliding underneath the seats..." he drawled, wriggling an arm in front of him in a serpentine pattern.

"Stop it."

"Maybe winding around your leg to get up higher and take a peek out the windows..." The arm continued to waver.

"Stop it!" I hit his arm with the back of my hand.

"What? Snakes like to look out windows." He made a hissing sound and I lunged at him, covering his mouth with my hand.

He laughed, the sound muffled by my palm, and grabbed me so tight to his side I went on my toes, shaking my hand away from his face so he could hiss again.

"Agh!" I hollered.

He couldn't hiss again, he was laughing too hard.

I shifted tactics, turning on the full puppy dog pout. "Please stop?"

He sighed, easing his grip on me so I sank back onto my heels. "Now that's cheating. Puppy face?"

"Desperate times call for desperate measures."

A semi truck rolled by us, kicking up road grit and making its own wind, which tossed my hair into my face, the ends also slapping Beckett.

He winced, and pushed my hair back, his palm gliding over my ear. "So, are we allowed to get back on the road?"

"I suppose."

"Good. Come on, wifey."

I cringed, but laughed. "Can we just stick with Emmy?"

"No way. I'm going to call you every terrible pet name I can think of. My better half, the little missus...ooh, the ol' ball and chain."

"Oh my god." I shoved him as we walked back toward the car, making him compensate with a few extra steps.

He cackled with satisfaction.

"I guess that makes you my old man?" I asked.

"I'll accept bae, king, or papa bear."

"I think I'm going to throw up."

Beckett grinned. We were at the car, and he thumbed the fob to unlock the doors. "Please do it before you get back in my car, okay?"

I rolled my eyes at him before I got in the passenger seat.

Beckett turned over the ignition. "Oh, that reminds me—" He killed the motor and pulled out the key, then reached across to unlock the glove compartment and dig around inside, emerging with a small black velvet box. "You should wear this."

"What is it?"

"A ring."

I levered the box open, finding a thin silver band with a row of four small diamonds. "You've been keeping a diamond ring in the fucking glove box?" I demanded.

"It was locked," he said, as if that were obvious.

"Diamond!" I repeated, turning it into three syllables.

"See if it fits." He turned the car on for the second time and backed out of his parking spot.

I was afraid to touch the ring, much less put it on my finger. "Was this the one for Emily?"

"Yeah."

I poked at it. "I feel weird about wearing her ring."

"Well I'm not getting you another one."

"No, I know that. I just…it was for her."

"The diamonds were my grandma's. It's just a new setting."

"That makes it worse!"

"Why?"

"It's a family heirloom and I'm your fake wife. I'd…I don't know, give it bad luck or something."

"Don't you think you should have a ring, though? We're supposed to be married."

"We *are* married."

"You know what I mean."

"I…I don't feel right about this." I closed the box and held it out to him.

"Emily's never going to wear it," he said sullenly, ignoring my offering.

"You don't know that."

He huffed in exasperation and kept his eyes fixed on the road. Eventually I let the ring box drop into my lap. Then, after a few minutes, I put it back in the glove box, wishing I could lock it away.

We didn't talk for a long time after that.

8

SHOUT IT OUT LOUD

*T*he upside to Beckett's frustration was that he kept his foot down hard on the accelerator. We flew across the remainder of Nebraska, eating up the road through half of Iowa before we called it quits for the night. Although the silence between us had eventually eroded into a more functional quiet, where we could still exchange words when necessary, we hadn't had a true conversation since the rest stop.

Beckett let me out of the car at the front door of another cheap motel and I got us a room for the night. Thank you, Dad. Beckett didn't speak when I told him which end of the building to park at, but after he'd pulled into the spot and killed the engine, he made no move to get out of the car.

Eyes still focused out the windshield, he said, "I get why you don't want to wear her ring."

"Thank you."

"Sorry I've been a dick."

"You weren't." He was, but I had been meeting his silence with my own, so what was I going to say? Besides, he was supposed to marry the love of his life yesterday and instead he'd married me. I guess I could understand why he'd be a little sensitive. "And you're right, I should have a ring. We both should."

He nodded.

For the first time I wondered if Emily had a ring for him. Where was it? Or had she not even bothered to get one, knowing in her heart she was going to call off the wedding.

"I'll get one," I told him. "You don't have to worry about it. Just, not that one, okay?"

He nodded again.

"Let's get our stuff inside."

We untangled our most important things from the back, making several trips to the room to get it all inside. The hotel room might as well have been a copy of the one we'd stayed in last night. It was laid out identically, except in mirror image.

"This is messing with my head," Beckett said.

"Seriously."

Once again, we took our turns in the bathroom, washing off a day of travel and getting into pajamas. I went second tonight, coming out of the bathroom with my hair still in a towel. Beckett was sitting on the bed I'd expected to have as my own for the night, and I did a double take.

"You switched."

"I needed to do something to stop the Twilight Zone feeling of this room."

I smiled at him. "Okay, but if you get confused in the middle of the night and get in bed with me, I reserve the right to kick you."

"Deal."

I bent over, unfurling my towel and scrubbing my scalp. Brown stands of wet hair whipped around as I scrubbed, sprinkling the cheap carpet with dots of water. When I straightened, I noticed Beckett had his forearm draped over his eyes.

"You okay?"

"When you bend over like that I can see down your shirt."

Heat rushed into my face like a firework bursting inside my head. "Oh."

"I didn't look," he said.

"Good." I shifted my feet awkwardly. "Could you turn off the light?"

He didn't question me, uncovering his eyes to flip the switch, plunging the room into darkness. I had to wait until my vision adjusted before I could get into bed.

Once I was safely under the covers, I felt like I could breathe again. The sound of rustling sheets told me Beckett was restless.

"Everything all right?" I asked.

"Yeah, sure." More rustling. A long silence, then more rustling. "I can't stop thinking about her tonight."

"Understandable."

"It's so fucked up. I don't even really miss her because I never fucking saw her. But in my head I *know* that I was supposed to be with her right now. We were going to get married, Em. *Married.*" He said it like it was something completely separate from what we did in Las Vegas. I guessed it was, when it came down to it.

"I'm sorry," I said quietly.

"I'm just so fucking pissed at her! I cannot believe she couldn't bother to tell me the fucking truth all this time. She *knew.* She knew she'd pulled out of Middlesex. She *knew* she'd signed up for classes at Arizona. The last time I saw her, she already *knew* all this and she lied to my face." His voice broke.

My heart clenched. "Beck, I'm so sorry."

His voice was barely audible over a wet breath. "Fuck."

I scrambled out of bed and stepped across to sit on the edge of his bed, my hands searching the dark for him. I found his torso under the sheets and worked my way up to his shoulders, leaning in and wrapping my arms around him. He stiffened at first, then pulled me tight to him, pulling my feet off the floor. In a blur of motion, I ended up on the bed beside him, my legs draped over his hip and his face buried in my neck. I couldn't see him, but the wetness of his tears on my skin and the sound of his hitching breath were all the evidence I needed that he was crying. My own eyes burned in sympathy.

"I'm so sorry," I repeated, holding on as if I could keep him from flying apart.

He mumbled something I couldn't understand, but his arms tightened around me. He wanted me there, that much I could tell. For as many days as I'd spent with him over the last week, I hadn't seen him cry. He'd seemed numb. Lost at times. Occasionally angry, or even despondent, but there were no tears until now.

I just held on as best I could, hoping it was enough. The air conditioning kicked on, making my bare legs rash in goosebumps until I started to shiver involuntarily. With a sudden gymnastic maneuver, Beckett yanked the blanket out from beneath me and swooped me under it with him. His body heat was a welcome relief and I gave one more mighty shiver as the cold started to leave me.

For a long time we stayed that way, huddled in each other's arms beneath a scratchy motel blanket, until Beck seemed to run out of tears.

"Better?" I asked, when his arms relaxed around me.

"No," he said miserably.

"Oh. Right."

He sighed. "I'm sorry, Em."

"Don't be."

"I've been trying really hard to keep it together, but..." He sighed again. "I can't stop thinking about it."

"Of course you can't, you idiot." I stroked his head, even though his short hair didn't really move under my hands. "It's all still new. And it's been a weird couple of days. I think it's okay that you're feeling a little off."

"Yeah."

"I'm sorry this is all happening at once. I wish you'd had more time to deal with Emily before you ended up stuck with me."

"It's not your fault."

"Yeah, but it still sucks."

He chuckled softly. "It really does. It really fucking sucks."

I smiled, even though he couldn't see me. "Does that make you feel better? Saying it out loud, I mean?"

"Sort of."

"Then say it again."

"This really fucking sucks."

"This sucks!" I agreed, raising my voice a bit.

"I'm not going louder," he said.

"Spoilsport."

There was a pause and then he hollered, *"This really fucking sucks!"* so loudly I jumped and slammed my hands over my ears.

Someone pounded on the wall above our heads and we both giggled.

"See?" I said, "It helps."

"Maybe a little."

It was so warm under the blankets, I could have easily gotten drowsy. It was clearly time to disentangle myself before I dozed off.

"All right, lemme up." I struggled free of our tangle and shivered in the cool room as I went back to my bed. "Get some sleep, okay?"

"Thanks, Emmy."

9

YOU HAVE BEEN ASSIMILATED

*T*he next day we got to sleep in a bit longer since there were only a couple hours left to get to River Glen. No point getting there at the crack of dawn when the housing office wouldn't even be open.

Beckett seemed more relaxed in the morning as we packed up the car for the last time. I wouldn't go so far as to say he looked happy, but he seemed to be in a better place than he'd been when we arrived at the hotel.

We got on the road mid-morning, and we were in River Glen by lunch time.

The town was small, and so unbelievably quaint I was pretty sure we'd run over Norman Rockwell if we weren't careful. There was a small downtown area with all one- and two-story buildings. Restaurants, cafes, and local shops lined the main street, and pedestrians milled along the sidewalks in the bright midday sun. There were dogs on leashes wagging their tails and giving doggy grins to everyone who passed. There were moms pushing strollers and business people out for their lunch breaks.

"Is this place for real?" I asked as we drove by a small park where kids swarmed the playground equipment and moms sat on benches with iced coffees in hand.

"Seriously. Do you think Andy Griffith is the sheriff here?"

"I'm positive he is."

Beckett drove slowly to let the foot traffic get safely from one place to another. I caught a few people looking at his car with mild interest. The California license plate was probably an unusual sight in this town.

After we passed out of the business district, we drove through a few residential areas on our way to the campus. The houses were as cute as downtown. Some of them had actual white picket fences.

I was seriously starting to wonder when the camera crew would appear. This was clearly a movie set.

The large, low stone wall with the brass letters spelling MIDDLESEX announced that we'd reached the edge of campus. We passed a few administrative and maintenance buildings before we hit the high wall that surrounded the main academic buildings. There was a large metal archway over the entrance to the tree-shaded main path through the green space. It was so god damn perfect, I asked Beckett to pull over so I could take a picture.

I sent it to Ash with the caption, *Have arrived in Pleasantville.*

Beckett followed the GPS to the Housing Office, which was only another mile away, and parked in a spot designated *15 minute parking only.* The RAV4's engine ticked in the silence after he turned it off.

"We're here," he said.

"Do you think they'll issue us 2.3 children and a golden retriever with our apartment?"

"It's entirely possible."

We climbed the short flight of stone steps to the entrance and went inside. There was a large wooden window on the wall opposite the doors with an older woman seated behind the counter there. A bulletin board hung beside the window, covered in notices and official posters. A wire basket sat on the counter with a sign labeled "Deposits."

The woman looked up with a pleasant smile. She was fair-skinned and gray-haired, with a welcoming face. The complete opposite of the woman at the chapel back in Vegas.

"Can I help you?"

Beckett and I approached. My heart began to pound with nervousness. This was it. The moment of truth.

"I'm Beckett Anderson," he said. "I'm here to pick up my keys?"

"Let me take a look." She had him spell his name and confirm his birth date while she clacked away at a computer on the counter. A few mouse clicks later, she said, "Okay I see you're assigned to apartment 203 in Overlook. There's a note here that says we're supposed to confirm your marital status. Would you happen to have that with you?"

"Yes," I said, holding out the temporary copy of our marriage license from Nevada. There would be an official one later, but the chapel staff had assured us this would do the same job until then. My hand shook slightly, making the page rattle, but she didn't seem to notice.

The woman took our form, looking it over carefully. "Oh, I see you're newlyweds!"

"Yeah," Beckett said.

"Congratulations!" She looked up at us with starry eyes. "Well, come on, let's see the ring!"

Just like that my stomach was in my shoes. But Beckett was ready. "We're getting it sized. It didn't fit quite right."

She nodded, looking sympathetic. "Oh, too bad."

My jaw quivered but I forced a smile that I hoped didn't look completely terrified. Beckett swung his arm around my shoulders, giving me a squeeze. "I guess driving across the country isn't the usual honeymoon, but it worked for Emmy and me."

"How wonderful!" she gushed.

"Nebraska was really flat." *What the actual fuck?* My eyes went wide in surprise. Those were my first words to this woman? What was wrong with me?

Beckett just gave me another squeeze. "Yeah, it was."

The woman laughed, delighted. "Well, we're sure happy you made it. Welcome to Middlesex. Let me get you your keys." She got up from her seat and went to a large locked cabinet across the office.

"Nebraska was really flat?" Beckett whispered softly.

"I don't know!" I hissed.

He chuckled. "That was perfect."

"Shut up." I shrugged my shoulders until his hand dropped away.

The woman returned with a set of keys and an envelope. She led us through a bit of administrative work, signing forms and showing our drivers' licenses to prove we were who we said we were. Then she handed over our lease agreement, a barely readable campus map with the route to our apartment highlighted, and gave us the keys.

"All right, you two," she said, "go get yourselves settled at Overlook. You're going to love it there. Lots of young couples just like you. And if you ever need anything, don't hesitate to call or stop by. I'm always here."

We went on our way, neither of us speaking until we were safely back in Beckett's car.

"Holy crap." I sagged in my seat. "She bought it."

"Man I was so nervous." Beckett confessed. Then he shot me a look. "Not, like 'Nebraska was really flat' nervous, but you know."

"Shut up!" I laughed and shoved him half-heartedly. "I can't believe you had an answer for the ring thing."

"I thought of it while we were in Nebraska." He paused. "Which was really flat, incidentally."

"Oh my god, I hate you." I covered my face with both hands. "I should un-marry you."

"Not yet," he said.

"Just drive, okay?"

He laughed and pulled onto the street.

Overlook wasn't far away or hard to find, and soon enough we were carrying our first load of stuff up from the car. Beckett unlocked the door and shoved it open.

Inside, the tiny apartment was utterly bare. Dark, industrial-strength carpet and dark woodwork. There was a kitchen with white counters in a U shape, leaving a small peninsula separating the living area from the food prep area. Through a door there was a small, empty square room featuring only a closet. Another door led to the small but functional bathroom, completely tiled in white walls with a brown speckled floor.

I turned slowly in a circle, taking it all in, my heart now racing again.

"There's only one bedroom," I said.

"Um, yeah."

"There's no furniture," I said.

"Nope."

"Uh, Beck...you didn't mention that there was only one bedroom."

"It's all they give to people with no kids."

"And the no furniture?"

"Surprise?"

"Oh my god."

"We should get the rest of our stuff. I'm parked in the loading zone."

"Oh my god."

"Focus, Emmy."

"Oh. My. God."

Beckett shook his head and turned back toward the hall. "Come help me when your brain reboots."

10

THE BARE NECESSITIES

*E*ventually I did help unload, because when faced with a weird situation, it's better to have something to do than nothing. It wasn't like it took very long to unload. We'd lived in a furnished apartment in California, and everything we owned had fit in a Toyota RAV4. Plus with no furniture, all we had to do was put everything on the floor in the living room.

After, we stood together in the living room surrounded by our things and I gave him an expectant look.

"Now what?"

"Uhh…"

Our front door was still standing open from the last load, and a figure appeared in it, tapping lightly on the jamb.

"Hello?" a female voice called. She was backlit by the hall, but she appeared to be around our age, maybe a few years older. Tall with curly red hair pulled up in a messy bun.

"Hello."

"Hi, I'm, um, Ginny?" she said uncertainly. "I live across the hall?"

I blinked at her vacantly for a moment before I remembered how to human. "Hi, I'm Emmy."

"Hi," she said again, taking a half step through the doorway. "I, uh, saw you guys carrying in your stuff and, oh wow, you have amazing eyes—" she did a double-take, interrupting herself. I was used to people commenting on my big green eyes, but it still never failed to make me want to blink a lot. Ginny came back to herself. "Anyway, I was wondering if you needed any help. Like with your furniture? My husband and I just moved in yesterday."

"Um…" I couldn't disguise the quaver in my voice. "We don't actually have any furniture."

"Oh!" Ginny flopped her arms once, helplessly. "Well, I guess I should have asked sooner then."

"We drove here from California," Beckett explained. "We didn't bring much with us."

"Wow, that must have been…long."

"Yeah. Hi, I'm Beckett." He stepped forward, offering his hand for her to shake, which prompted me to do the same thing. Why was he so much better at being a person than me right now?

"So, um, you wouldn't happen to know a good place where we could get some furniture, would you?" I asked.

Ginny laughed. "Well, Tom and I found a Walmart down the road, but I'm not sure they're going to have everything you need."

"It's a start," Beckett said. "We don't even have toilet paper."

I looked at him in horror. "Oh my god, we don't."

"Tell you what, why don't you guys go get what you need, and maybe we could have you over for dinner tonight?" She sounded downright scared at making the offer. I could totally respect that level of introversion.

For some reason, tears pricked at my eyes. "That's really nice of you."

She looked relieved. "Great. I'll let you get on your way, and we'll see you later."

We thanked her and she left us alone in the apartment.

"So, should we make a list?" Beckett asked, looking around the room.

"Pretty sure we need one of everything," I said. "Maybe two of everything."

"Right." He gestured for me to go out the front door.

"And remember I'm broke."

"Right."

"I'll pay you back."

"It's okay."

"No really." We took the stairs side-by-side.

"It's really okay."

At the main building door, I added, "And we have to get the good toilet paper."

"Whatever you say, wifey."

"Stop that."

"Yes, dear."

I gave him dagger eyes, but he just grinned.

Back in California, Mary had been our unofficial house mother. She was always the one who remembered to put things on the house list when we ran out. Things like toilet paper, dish soap, and coffee. And we all chipped in every time she went out to get us what we needed. Sure, I shopped for groceries when I needed them, but it had been a long time since I'd had to be responsible for all the household necessities. And when I say a long time, I pretty much mean never.

So when Beckett and I found ourselves pushing a cart up and down the aisles of the Walmart Ginny had mentioned, I nearly had a breakdown in the cleaning products aisle. There were so many cleaning sprays to choose from. Some said Bathroom, some said Kitchen, some said All-Purpose. And after we managed to find the one that Mary usually bought, it occurred to me that we'd need something to wipe the spray with. We had no broom, no dish rack. Not even a sponge.

"How are we supposed to do this? Why is this so hard?" I asked.

"We should have brought Mary with us," Beckett said, pushing the cart around a corner.

"Oh Jesus, hand soap!" I wailed, seeing the display in the next aisle.

"Do we really need all this crap?" He peered into the cart, already half full. "Maybe we need to go back to the basics."

"Hand soap is pretty basic, Beck."

"I guess."

Aisle after aisle we discovered all the things we did not own. Our last apartment had even had dishes in the cabinets when we arrived. Neither of us had a fork or a plate to our names. We stood in the dishware section, looking at color after color and pattern after pattern. Boxed sets, service for 8 or 12.

"Maybe we should just get paper plates."

My instant reaction was to tell him what a dumb idea that was, but looking at the heap of items in our cart already, the thought died. "Yeah, okay. We'll get plates another time."

So it went, through the store. Decision after decision. So much *stuff*. How had I graduated from college without having a clue how much stuff it took to survive?

In the furniture section, we realized we could get a few things here, but we had no idea how we'd fit it in the back of Beckett's car. There was a lot of standing around, tilting our heads at various flatpack boxes.

"We could get a futon," I suggested. "For the living room?"

Beckett toed the huge box on the bottom shelf. "It's not a bad idea, but I literally don't know how we'd get it home."

"Right."

So we did what any twenty-two-year-olds with no real life experience would do: Nothing. We just left.

We hit another roadblock when we reached the food section, and realized we didn't have anything to eat either.

Beckett looked at me. "Ginny is feeding us tonight, right? Do we have to get food?"

"Um…" This time my gut reaction was to say no. I didn't want to spent another half hour picking out food. But then I remembered that we were going to wake up tomorrow in our brand new apartment and not have a single thing to eat. "Maybe some toaster waffles?" I suggested.

"We don't have a toaster," he reminded me.

"Right. Okay. Um…"

Beckett scanned the signs at the ends of the aisles and suddenly set off in a determined fashion. He led us to the breakfast cereal section and proudly picked up a box of Frosted Mini Wheats.

"We don't have bowls," I said.

"Fuck."

"We'll eat it out of the box."

"No milk?"

I threw up my hands in exasperation. "Okay, tomorrow we go out for Egg McMuffins. *Then* we'll figure the food part out."

"Deal." He started pushing the cart toward the check-out, and I trailed behind, looking longingly down the cookie aisle for a second. *Some Oreos might help my existential angst right now*, I thought.

"Emmy!" Beckett's voice drew my attention and I realized he'd gotten out of sight. I hurried to catch up and found him near the edge of the women's clothing department.

"Sorry! There were cookies…"

"Rings," he said, pointing at the jewelry case up ahead.

"Oh."

We rolled closer and peered into the glass display. I'd never looked at Walmart jewelry before, and I was shocked to see a display of rings with a cardboard cutout of wedding bells mounted behind it.

"Score," Beckett said.

We had to wait for an employee to notice us lingering there, and it took a lot longer than I expected, so we had plenty of time to decide which rings we wanted to see. The man who finally unlocked the case and pulled the tray out looked completely bored with life.

"How much is this one?" I asked, pointing to a thin band with a series of clear stones on it. It resembled the one that was destined for Emily, but it was different enough that I didn't feel weird about it.

The bored guy plucked it out of the display and used the plastic price gun on his belt to scan the bar code.

"Twenty-nine ninety-five," he said.

"Sold," I told him.

"What size?"

I had no idea, and he had to call a manager over to figure out how to size my finger. This was followed by a long search through a hidden cabinet behind the counter to find the ring I was looking for in my size. And then we repeated the whole thing with the plain silver band that Beckett wanted. Bored, I studied the box my ring came in, and burst into laughter.

"What?" Beckett asked.

"This ring is called a Semi-Eternity ring!"

He got it right away and let out a bark of laughter. The employees looked at us like we'd lost our minds, but we could not stop laughing. I could not think of anything more perfect for our fake marriage than a semi-eternity ring.

Eventually we got control of ourselves and Beckett managed to get the right ring. But we both kept getting the giggles while they searched for it. We were still grinning at each other like loons when we checked out, letting the cashier wonder exactly what kind of drugs we might be on.

We loaded the car with our unexpected necessities and made our way back to Overlook, carrying everything upstairs in two trips.

"Still no bed," I pointed out.

"Yep," he agreed.

"Are we sleeping on the floor tonight?"

"Looks that way." He frowned. "But on the bright side, we have hand soap."

"That's true." I put one finger in the air. "And the good toilet paper."

For the next hour, we went through our meager possessions, putting away what we could—not much—and sorting the rest into sections. The bedroom became the place where we put all the clothes and blankets and pillows and such. The living room was home to our electronics and random books and things. The hand soap went on the edge of the kitchen sink, and I was going to hang the shower curtain we'd remembered to buy, but it turned out that we didn't buy shower curtain hooks.

A knock on the door diverted my attention from the problem and I found Ginny waiting nervously in the hall.

"Hi, sorry to bother you. It turns out there's going to be a big barbecue in the community area out back later. So, I was thinking maybe we could reschedule dinner for another night?"

"Oh. Sure. That sounds fine." As long as someone was going to feed us, it was all right with me.

"Did you guys find what you needed?" she asked, trying to look over my shoulder without being obvious, which was a complete failure.

I threw the door wide open. "Still no furniture," I said. "Turns out a small SUV is not conducive to bringing home a couch."

She laughed. "No, I guess not. Did you guys see the notice board downstairs? I think there are a few people trying to get rid of some furniture."

"No! Where?"

Ginny told me where to find it and I took off without a word to Beckett.

She was right, there were a number of hand-written signs up with people looking to offload things. I tore them all off the board and ran upstairs.

I was about to save the day.

11

EMMY AND BECK'S DOWN HOME
WEDDIN' BBQ

*B*y the time we were ready for the community barbecue, not only had we met a number of other people in the building, we'd acquired a hodge-podge of their unwanted belongings. So now we were the proud owners of: one small, wobbly table and three wooden chairs that all squeaked when you sat down; two completely mismatched night stands, one blue and one covered in mirrors; one floor lamp; four table lamps, none of which were the same; a desk chair; and best of all —a futon. A glorious metal futon that was going to mean I didn't have to sleep on the floor that night.

I was feeling quite pleased with myself. Although I also felt quite grubby, since we'd spent hours carrying furniture and still didn't have hooks to hang our shower curtain. I did my best, putting on clean clothes and washing my face, but I had definitely felt more presentable in my life.

Before we left, Beckett held out the little white box labeled Semi-Eternity. "Suit up," he said. He had his own box in his other hand. We unwrapped them together and I held mine pinched between two fingers.

"Is this weird?" I asked. "It feels a little weird."

"It's weird."

We looked at each other for a moment. I bit my lip, and then offered my ring to him. He gave a little nod and took it from me. I held out my left hand and he slid the ring onto my third finger, then gave me his ring. I put his on, feeling a strange electric shiver run through me. Somehow this felt more symbolic than the actual ceremony had been. Like we were actually officially married now.

"So, that's it, then."

"I guess so." Beckett looked at his hand for a minute. "I hope this doesn't turn my finger green."

I gasped with fake shock. "How dare you insult my ring! This has been in my family for years!"

He grinned. "Uh huh."

"All right, come on, hubs. Let's go make like we like each other."

We were among the last to arrive at the barbecue in the big grassy area behind the building. And as soon as we arrived, I could see that we were also probably the only people who didn't bring a contribution to the feast.

"Oh god, we're the tacky ones," I said under my breath.

"It's fine. We just got here, Em."

"We should have at least brought beer."

"Ugh. Beer." Beckett slapped his forehead. "That should have been the first item on our list today. Fuck the hand soap."

Ginny spotted us and waved from across the yard. There was a very tall man with her, with sandy blond hair and glasses.

"Hey you guys!" she called as we approached. "This is my husband, Tom."

We did the introduction thing. Yes, we drove all the way from California. Yes, just got here today. Yes, that's right, we didn't have any furniture.

"So do you have a moving van on the way with the rest of your stuff?" Tom asked.

"No." I shook my head, my cheeks growing warm. "We don't have any."

His eyes widened. "Oh. Wait—how long have you been married?"

We looked at each other, and Beckett answered. "Two days."

That was all it took. Ginny and Tom could literally not believe it. They dragged us over to every other person they'd met in the building to tell them all that there were newlyweds among us. And the reaction was the same every time. They were all shocked that we'd come to Iowa, that we hadn't had a honeymoon. That our wedding night had been spent in a cheap hotel in Colorado. That we'd only lived in a furnished college apartment before this.

Within a half hour, I'm pretty sure we were the unofficial mascots of Overlook. I showed my thirty-dollar wedding ring off time and again as they demanded to see it. Our neighbors were either all very polite, or the cheap jewelry was better looking than I thought, because everyone complimented it.

I apologized for not bringing anything to the barbecue, but the apology fell on deaf ears. The famous Midwestern niceness was almost overwhelming. They all wanted to do for us. Bring us food. Get us drinks. Offer to show us around town. And give us plenty of marriage advice.

When the clinking sound began, I didn't know what to make of it, but it slowly got louder and louder until there was no ignoring it. I noticed everyone was looking at us with excitement in their eyes.

"Kiss her!" someone shouted, and the reality crashed home. It was the wedding reception thing. People were clinking their bottles of beer to get the bride and groom to kiss.

The bride and groom in this case just happened to be me and my fake husband.

"Kiss the bride!" someone else called out.

Beckett looked at me with the question all over his face, *What do we do now?*

I gave him a tiny shrug, but reached out my hand toward him. *It's okay*, I wanted to say. *We can do this.*

He took my hand and stepped closer, bending to meet my lips with his. It was a dry, closed-lip kiss, just like the one at the chapel in Vegas.

"Boo! You call that a kiss?" a voice called.

Beckett released my hand to curve his arm around my waist and pull me close. He looked into my eyes for a second before leaning in for another kiss. This one wasn't so chaste. His lips urged mine to part, and my pulse rushed as I felt the barest sweep of his tongue. If you'd asked me a week ago if I thought I'd ever have my friend Beckett's tongue in my mouth, the answer would have been a firm no. But to my shock, it wasn't as weird as I would have thought.

I mean, it was weird. But it wasn't gross, or bad. Just…new.

It was our first real kiss, but it wouldn't be the last for the evening. The community of Overlook seemed galvanized by the idea of the newlyweds in the yard, and they seemed to all silently agree that this would be our ad hoc wedding reception. The glass clinking happened again just a few minutes later when we'd both drifted into separate conversations with our new neighbors.

"Go on!" the woman I was talking to urged, waving her hand in dismissal. "Give the people what they want."

I found Beckett and kissed him, taking the lead this time, on tiptoe with my arms wrapped around his neck. I gave him a hard, cartoonish kiss that made everyone laugh, including us when I pulled back. Beckett rubbed his lips.

"Ow," he said. "Ease up there, killer."

"Sorry." I sank back to my feet. "I'm just so hot for you."

He laughed, unwinding my arms from his neck. "I mean, who can blame you?"

The same thing happened over and over. We'd drift apart, or he'd cross the yard to get a beer and suddenly someone would get the bright idea that it was time for another kiss from the newlyweds. The bottles clinked, and we'd drop what we were doing to meet in the middle of the yard for another kiss.

In a way, it was like jumping into the deep end of the pool. Nothing takes the awkwardness out of kissing your fake husband like having to do it ten times in the span of a couple hours.

Also, it turns out that kissing someone *a lot* breaks down other barriers. By the end of the party, I felt more comfortable when Beckett put his arm around my shoulders, or rested his hand on the small of my back. And it seemed natural that when I wanted to get his attention, I stroked my hand down his forearm.

We were going to be so great at this fake marriage thing. We definitely had everyone at the party fooled.

I wondered if I should feel bad for fooling them. They were all lovely people. Lots of students from other countries, and couples with new babies or little kids. We were young compared to a lot of them, but that didn't seem to matter. I got invited to join a book club, go to a yoga class, and attend a leggings party—I wasn't sure what that last one was. Part of me wanted to burst out with the truth. Just say, "Oh, and by the way, we only got married for the apartment. Just so you know." But I didn't.

As the sky darkened, the families with kids began to say their goodbyes. And it wasn't too long before the gathering seemed to lose steam. Eventually we stood with Ginny and Tom, sipping our beers and slapping away mosquitos. Iowa had a lot of mosquitos. Who knew?

"You guys must be exhausted," Ginny said.

"It's been a long day," I agreed.

"And tomorrow won't be any shorter," Beckett said. "We still have a lot to do."

"Like get some of those things to hang the stupid shower curtain." I made my thumb and ring finger into a circular shape.

"Like that."

We chatted for a few more minutes, but my intermittent yawning seemed to be a sign to Ginny. "Come on, let's get you guys inside." She led the way into the building and up to the second floor. The apartment doors were staggered slightly, but ours was as close to directly across from theirs as it could be, so we were with Ginny and Tom until the last second.

"Well, good night. It was great meeting you," I said.

"If there's anything you need," Tom said, "let us know."

"I think we'll be okay for the night, but thanks." Beckett said, looking up after he unlocked the door. It was pitch dark inside. We hadn't thought to leave any lights on.

"Enjoy your first night in the new place," Ginny said, then her eyes widened. "Wait, aren't you supposed to carry her across the threshold?"

"Uhh..." Beckett looked at me for help.

"Oh Gin, leave them alone," Tom chided.

I flapped a dismissive hand. "We've been going in and out all day. I think the moment has passed."

She laughed, shaking her head. "You're right. Sorry. I get a little excited."

"Ginny loves weddings," Tom said, putting his arm around his wife's shoulders, and she blushed.

Beckett glanced at me, then Ginny and Tom, and back at me. "Come on, Emmy." He beckoned me with both hands.

I stepped slowly closer and he suddenly scooped me off my feet into a cradle hold. I squealed in shock and wrapped my arms around his neck for safety. Beckett laughed and turned his body to angle my feet through the dark doorway.

Behind us, Ginny made a soft, approving noise and Tom laughed.

Beckett managed to get me through the door without smacking my head on the frame, which I appreciated a lot. Once inside, he turned quickly, making me squeal again and cling tighter to him.

"There," he said, clearly for Ginny's benefit. "Threshold crossed."

"Yay!" Ginny golf clapped. "Have a good night, Mr. and Mrs. Anderson."

"Good night," Beckett said. "Em, grab the door."

I cautiously released one hand from his shoulder and swung the door shut, calling, "Good night!"

When it clicked home, we were plunged into complete darkness. Beckett let me down to my feet slowly, but we stayed close together, clinging to each other until we each had a hold of our cell phones to use for light.

It was just enough illumination to avoid tripping over the stuff scattered on the floor until Beckett found one of the table lamps and cast a pale amber glow across the the living room. The bulb had come with the lamp, and it seemed to be a 15-watt at best. The light was barely enough to read by, but it kept me from tripping.

"I feel so gross," I told Beckett. "I can't believe I have to sleep like this."

He thought for a moment. "I have an idea." He disappeared into the bathroom and I heard the sound of vinyl crinkling. After a few minutes, he called, "I need something to hold this!"

In the bathroom, I found him holding the shower curtain over the rod like a towel hanging up to dry. It was uneven, with just a few inches bent over the rod, and the rest draped down to the top of the tub. He couldn't let go or the whole thing would collapse.

"Ideas?" he said.

I racked my brain, dismissing a few bad ideas, like staples, and safety pins, before scurrying out to the living room and dredging up a roll of duct tape. When I returned, brandishing it like a prize, Beckett grinned.

"Ta da!"

"Brilliant."

I pulled off strips of tape and together we got the temporary fix in place.

"Wow," I said when we stepped back to admire our work. "That looks terrible."

"Hey, do you want to shower or not?" Beckett asked.

"Shower."

"Okay then. You can go first."

It took a little searching by dim lamplight to find a towel and my shampoo, but it was worth it. That was one of the best damn showers of my life. I felt so much better by the time I got out, towel turban twisted around my hair and clean shorts and a t-shirt for sleeping on my ready-for-bed body.

Beckett was sitting in the lone desk chair, slowly spinning it while he looked at his phone.

"It's all yours," I said.

"I'll sleep on the floor tonight," he said without looking up.

"Huh?"

"You can have the futon. I'll take the floor."

"Beck..." My gut reaction was to protest, but at the same time, I really, really didn't want to sleep on the floor.

"It's fine. I don't mind." He stilled the chair with his feet and looked up at me, blinking a few times as the lack of motion caught up with him.

"You don't have to do that."

"I know. I'm offering."

"Okay, but tomorrow, you can have it."

"Deal." He stood and headed for the bathroom, not even breaking stride when he held up his hand for me to slap as he passed.

I found my pillow and a blanket, which I folded myself into taco style on the futon. I was too tired to find sheets, much less put them on. This would do for the night.

By the time Beckett got out of the bathroom, I was already asleep.

ONE BED TO RULE THEM ALL

*I*n the morning, Beckett came stumbling out of the bedroom with his hand braced on his lower back and announced that we had to do something about the furniture situation immediately. We spent that day and the next scouring Craigslist, flyers in the housing office and the student union, and browsing at a thrift shop. We borrowed bungee cords from Tom, and made a return trip to the Walmart to get a mattress and some rope to tie it to the roof—not to mention the shower curtain rings. And in one memorable hour, we carried a dresser four blocks, stopping to catch our breath and rearrange our grips about every ten steps.

They were two of the most grueling days of my life, but by the end, we had something resembling a real apartment. It was, admittedly, spartan. But there was no duct tape on the shower curtain anymore, and there was a real live bed in the bedroom with a mattress and everything.

Tom helped carry the mattress up the stairs, which made me want to cry with relief. It was covered in plastic when he and Beckett set it down on the platform frame we'd found on

Craigslist, but I couldn't wait. I crawled onto it, crunching, stiff plastic and all, and flopped down on my back with a huge sigh.

"A bed!" I crowed. "A for-real bed!"

Beckett crashed down beside me like a tree falling in the woods and the two of us lay there, cackling like hyenas while Tom looked on, shaking his head.

"Up top," Beckett said, holding his palm high above me. I slapped it and let my arm collapse back to the bed with another sigh.

"You need any other help right now?" Tom asked.

"Nope," Beckett said. "I'm never moving again." He lifted his head enough to look at our neighbor. "Thanks, man."

"No problem. I'll be across the hall if you have anything else you need help carrying."

"Thank you so much, Tom. Seriously. You've been so good to us." I knew I should get up and be polite. Thank him properly, or give the man a hug. He'd helped us with so much. Even the stupid dresser we'd carried for four blocks. By the time we'd arrived at the building, my arms were too shot to carry it up the stairs. Tom to the rescue. "I swear to god, I will learn how to make a cake just for you."

He chuckled. "No need. Although I never say no to cake."

"Cake it is!" I declared, still not making any moves to get off the plastic-wrapped mattress.

"I like cake," Beckett said in a pouty voice. "Why does he get all the cake?"

"Hypothetical cakes for everyone!" I was feeling grandiose with brand new mattress coils beneath me. "If I ever get up again."

"Good point." Beckett lifted his head to look at Tom again. "If you don't hear anything from us for a while, we'll probably be right here."

Tom shook his head, muttering, "Newlyweds," as he wandered out of the room.

"No, that's not—" I started to protest, but I quickly realized I couldn't. That was our cover. As far as the rest of the building was concerned, we were probably humping like rabbits in spring at every opportunity.

The sound of the front door opening and closing told us Tom was gone.

"So, what? Do we rock-paper-scissors for the bed?" Beckett asked, holding up a fist.

"Don't be silly." I turned my head to look at him with big innocent doe eyes. My already big eyes could be downright cartoonish if I widened them far enough. "I told you last night that the futon was all yours tonight."

"Oh you little—" He lunged at me, digging his fingers into my ribs. I screamed and grabbed his wrists and tried to get away, but he was stronger than me. Although to be fair, I was also helplessly convulsing with laughter, which made escape more challenging.

He didn't let up until I was completely out of breath and tears were streaming down my face. "Stop!" I gasped. "Gonna pee!"

Instantly his fingers vanished from my body. "Do not pee on our brand new bed."

I grinned. "*My* brand new bed."

He made another half-hearted lunge for me, but I scooted off the bed and ran for the bathroom, giggling reflexively at the very idea of more tickling. I really did have to pee.

When I was no longer in danger of destroying our new property, I returned to the bedroom to find Beckett still sprawled on the bed, his eyes now half closed with impending sleep.

"I don't think so." I climbed onto the thick plastic and straddled his stomach, pinning his wrists before he realized what I was up to. "No falling asleep until we work this out."

"You seriously think you can hold me here?" he asked mildly.

I made a wet, hocking sound in the back of my throat and his eyes went as wide as saucers.

"No fucking way." The very thought of dangling spit seemed to give him super-human strength because I suddenly found myself on my back, arms pinned above my head and my legs flailing on either side of him.

"What the hell?" It had all happened so fast, I might as well have teleported here.

"My brother used to do that spit thing and I *hate* it."

I laughed and tried to wiggle free, but he had me so awkwardly positioned there was no hope.

"I wasn't actually going to do it," I said. "It was a joke." My hips were tilted so that I couldn't put my legs down, or really anywhere but around his waist, which I finally did just to steady myself.

"Not funny." His sweat-slicked skin lost purchase on the plastic covering the mattress, causing one hand to slide out, and Beckett to nearly fall on top of me. I flinched, thinking I was about to get unintentionally head-butted, but he caught himself with his face only an inch from mine. When the hit didn't come, I opened my eyes slowly.

We both let out relieved laughs.

"That was close," I said.

"Would have served you right for spitting on me."

"I wasn't going to do it!" I thumped my heel into his butt.

"Hey!" He tried to get back to his hands and knees but slipped again on the plastic, this time landing on me. We didn't butt heads, but his weight stole my breath. His grip slacked on my wrists and I felt the light scrape of his unshaven cheek against mine. It had been a while since I'd been on my back with a guy between my legs and for a second—less than a second even—I wished he would stay.

Though I couldn't really breathe, so on second thought...

I pushed at his shoulders until he rolled away from me, sitting on the edge of the bed with his back to me. Air rushed back into my lungs.

"You okay?" he asked.

"Fine," I wheezed.

"Good." He looked over his shoulder at me. "Because you know if you die, they'll definitely blame me. They always look at the husband first."

"I'd like to point out that this would have actually been your fault."

"I would tell the jury that you were threatening me with dangling spit and they would dismiss the charges immediately."

"Shut up." I planted one foot on his back and gave him a shove.

"And they'd award me the bed as compensation for my pain and suffering."

"You wouldn't even give me the bed if you killed me?"

"You'd be dead! What would you use it for?"

"My final resting place." I closed my eyes, and folded my hands over my chest, my toes stuck stiffly into the air.

Beckett eyed me skeptically for a moment. "Nope," he declared. "You're dead, you can sleep on the futon." And with that, he circled the bed and scooped me up in his arms. It was an echo of our fake threshold carry for Ginny, only this time, he carried me out of the bedroom, put me down with much less care than he'd done the first time, and closed the door behind me.

"Jerk!" I shouted.

"We'll take turns," he called back.

"So when's it my turn?"

"I'll let you know."

13

WON'T YOU STAY?

*I*t wasn't my turn for the entire month of September, apparently. As the heat of the late Iowa summer faded, life settled into something resembling a routine. Our days were dedicated to lectures on medical terminology, anatomy, physiology, and microscopy. Our evenings were consumed by studying, getting to know our fellow pathology classmates, and the endless project that was getting our apartment into some kind of livable condition. None of these activities seemed to end with me getting a turn in the bedroom.

Somewhere along the way, our crappy little apartment became the hub for the Pathologists' Assistant students. Seemed like a lot of other people's roommates were not that excited by groups of people hanging around in their living rooms drilling each other on microscopic anatomy and shouting out medical terminology. Beck and I were the only people who didn't live with so-called "normal" people who were grossed out by what we were all studying.

All of which meant that on any given evening, my bed was occupied by four other people's butts. I had to strip off my sheets and blankets every day and stash them in the bedroom so we could keep up the appearance that we were happy newlyweds. It wouldn't do at all to have the little missus sleeping on the couch, now would it?

On the plus side, being hangout central meant there was often leftover pizza and beer in our refrigerator. On the minus side, this also meant that I couldn't go to bed until everyone had given up on cramming facts into their heads for the night.

Overall, it wasn't a terrible life. Not by a long shot. The rest of the PA class turned out to be around our age, give or take a few years. And with all of us going through the same intense class schedule, we were sort of instantly bonded. None of us could afford to have much of a social life with all the classroom time, lab work, and studying we did. So we pretty much socialized with each other. Plus, Beckett and I had Ginny and Tom across the hall to provide a bit of "normal people" time, as we came to call it. They were the only people in our lives who weren't constantly thinking about human anatomy and physiology.

Then came the glorious day in October when I got the news that the bank had concluded the fraud investigation, and put my money back into my bank account. I actually burst into tears, I was so damn happy.

I ran up the stairs to our apartment, the letter clutched in my hands, and shook it at Beckett as I burst into the living room.

"I got my money back!"

He understood immediately and opened his arms to catch me as I ran to him. He spun me in a circle, my feet off the ground. "That's great!"

"Oh my god, I can't believe it!" I said as he put me back on the ground. I rattled the letter at him. "Look!"

"Did you check your balance yet?"

I shook my head, but immediately dug my phone out of my pocket to check if the deposit had arrived. Beckett kept one arm around my waist, leaning in with me to watch intently as the little loading circle slowly turned blue. Then, it was there, in all its comma-bearing glory. All the money I had worked my entire undergraduate career to save for grad school. Every penny that was meant for me to live on while I went to school full-time.

I grinned at Beckett. "It's here!"

"Hell yeah!" He gave me a one-armed squeeze and kissed my temple. "I'm really happy for you, Emmy."

Which of course made me start crying again. It wasn't any one thing. It was everything. Relief, happiness, frustration that it had taken this long, everything Beckett had done for me in the last six weeks, and the fact that now my major life disaster was solved, but his wasn't.

"I don't know what I would have done without you since we left California." I put my phone away and gave him a hug. "Thank you."

"I don't know what I would have done without you either," he said, rubbing one hand on my back as we stood together. "And... look, I know we said that this was—"

"Knock, knock!" A voice interrupted us from the front door, which I'd left hanging wide open as I sprinted through the apartment.

"Oh god, would you two get a fucking room?" A second voice added.

We released each other, and I turned to see three of our classmates coming through the door.

"We have a fucking room," Beckett told them. "You're in our fucking room, remember?"

"Well then you are fucking perverts for leaving the door open," said Jon, the owner of the second voice. He was perfectly cheerful about it, walking across the living area as if he owned the place and setting a six-pack of hard lemonade on the kitchen counter. His backpack was slung over one shoulder, obviously heavy with text books.

"We did say six, didn't we?" Mandy asked, following Jon to drop her own six-pack of IPA on the counter.

"Yeah." I glanced at my watch. "You're right on time."

"Then I guess you should have finished knocking boots before we got here." Jon could never resist a chance to rag on someone.

"Or at least closed the door," Reina spoke for the first time.

Over the next ten minutes, the rest of our classmates arrived for the nightly cram session. Tonight being a Friday, however, it was a little heavier on the pizza and beer than school nights. After a few hours, we gave up studying altogether to watch an American Ninja Warrior marathon and pay more thorough attention to the supply of beer than we'd allowed ourselves to do before.

I was the happiest I'd been in a long time as I sat back on the futon with my bottle of hard lemonade propped between my knees. With my bank account back in the black, a huge invisible weight was lifted off my shoulders. I was able to truly relax and enjoy being with my new friends.

There was an energy to being with a group of people who were all into the same not-around-the-dinner-table kind of stuff that I'd been into all my life. It's hard to be a girl who's fascinated by dissecting dead animals in science class, and who single-mindedly pursues a career that would put me full time in a morgue. Most people are not into acknowledging that death happens, much less basing their lives around it. So it was an eye-opening experience to be surrounded by people who felt the same way. Who weren't grossed out by talking about blood while we ate pizza covered in crimson sauce.

Of course, Beckett and I had always been able to talk "gross biology stuff," as our California roommates had called it. But we were only allowed to when none of them could hear us. And it wasn't like it came up as often in undergrad. Now he was next to me on the futon, his arm around my shoulders to make room for other people to squeeze in beside us. It had been a little odd to get used to being like this with him, but we did what we had to do to maintain our cover. It would have been weirder for him to sit next to his wife and not touch her.

I didn't even really mind him touching me. I was practically immune to it most of the time. After the endless showy kisses we'd given everyone at the welcome barbecue, it wasn't so hard to deal with a simple hand on my waist, or the random kiss on top of my head as he walked behind my chair. But there were still certain things that we didn't do. Lines we didn't cross. Body parts that stayed off-limits. His hands never went below my waist level. Mine never lingered more than a few seconds on his chest. We never touched each other's faces. We hadn't kissed on the lips since the barbecue. It was enough to feed the illusion that we were happily married, and that was it.

So imagine my surprise when I was startled awake by Beckett scooping me into his arms and lifting me from the couch.

"Wha—what's wrong?" I mumbled, clamping my arm around his neck for safety.

"Shh, nothing. You fell asleep," he whispered.

"Where are you—?"

From a distance I heard someone say softly, "Good night, Emmy," and I realized that there were still other people in our apartment.

Beckett carried me into the dark bedroom, where my sheets and blankets were still folded on the end of the bed. He lowered me to the bed, on top of the comforter, and grabbed one of my blankets to cover me with.

"I'm sorry," I murmured, "I didn't mean to…"

"It's okay," he said, "Just go back to sleep."

I didn't bother to protest, curling onto my side and tucking the blanket under my chin with both hands. Then, as is often the case with these things, my sleepiness faded a bit as my eyes adjusted to the dark. I watched as Beckett became a silhouette in the door, and heard a burst of laughter from the living room from the others.

"Beckett?" I said.

He turned, but he was backlit, so I couldn't see his face. "Yeah?"

"I know I said I'd get my own place after my money came back…"

"Yeah."

"But I was wondering if…do you want me to move out?"

He closed the door, sealing us together in the bedroom. "If you move out, I can't stay here either, remember?"

"So…?"

Now he took a few steps closer, leaning against the end of the bed. "So stay."

"Yeah?"

"Yeah."

"Okay, good."

I sensed his smile more than I could see it in the dark room.

"Now are you going to sleep or are you going to make me look like an asshole for carrying you in here?"

"Sleep."

"Okay then. I'll let you know when everyone is gone."

I nodded and he left the room, closing the door softly behind him. And when he was gone, I slithered out from my blanket, changed into my pajamas and got under the sheets.

Some time later, he came back in the room, the sound of the door startling me just enough to make me aware of his presence.

"Em," he whispered, coming close enough to shake me gently by the shoulder. "Em, they're gone."

I didn't even open my eyes, just burrowed deeper into the pillow and said, "It's my turn."

14

A LITTLE TOO EASY LIKE SUNDAY MORNING

*A*shley and I tried to talk to each other once a week, but even that could be a challenge. It was amazing that someone I shared a room with for two years, and saw every single day of my life could so quickly become hard to find even fifteen minutes with. We sent each other stupid Snaps almost every day, but it wasn't the same as talking.

It seemed like there was just never time. Between all my classes and how much time I spent studying in the evening, I had basically no life. Ashley was working as a concierge for one of the monster casinos on the Las Vegas strip, and as the new girl, she got the shittiest hours. So our schedules rarely lined up.

One Sunday morning in late October, my phone rang at seven a.m. I blearily searched for it, already planning the horrible things I was going to say to the telemarketer on the other end when I saw that not only was it Ashley, but she was on FaceTime. I couldn't imagine how horrible I must look, but it wasn't like she'd never seen me first thing, so I accepted the call.

"Oh shit, were you asleep?" she asked when the screen popped to life.

"Uh, yeah."

"I'm sorry! I keep forgetting about the time difference."

I double-checked the time and looked at her in confusion. "Isn't it five a.m. there?"

"Yeah!" she said brightly.

I wanted to ask her what the hell time she thought she was calling me at, because as far as I was concerned the hours between four and nine a.m. were strictly for emergencies. But I was still too tired to get all that straightened out in my head. So I just shook my head. "What are you doing up?"

"I haven't gone to bed yet," she said.

All I could do was groan.

"You know how it is when you're drinking champagne." Ashley grinned, and gave her shoulders a little shimmy. "It's better than an energy drink."

I rubbed my eyes with my free hand, trying to remember the last time I'd had champagne. Or stayed out all night. Or even gone out at all.

"How's Beck?" Ash asked. "Is he up? Let me say hi."

"It's seven o'clock in the morning," I reminded her.

"So? Wake him up!"

Fine, I thought. If I had to be awake, he could be too. "Hang on," I told her. I slithered out of bed and set the phone down to pull on my UC-Irvine sweatshirt before venturing into the living room. It was only October and already I was cold all the time. I was dreading the Iowa winter so hard.

Out in the living room, Beckett was sprawled on the futon like Spiderman clinging to a wall. The cold didn't seem to be affecting him too much yet, which was weird considering he was from Arizona, but he still wasn't even sleeping with a shirt on. He'd managed to thrash the blankets down to his waist while he slept, leaving his entire back exposed to the air. I had to admit, it was a very nice back. He'd been talked into joining a gym with a few of the other pathology guys, and the high-intensity workouts were paying off.

I tapped the screen to reverse the camera and show Ashley his prone form.

"See?" I whispered. "He's asleep."

She let out an ear-splitting whistle, and a wolfish growl. "Beck-ett, lookin' good, my man!"

He startled, slapping one hand over his ear. "What the—?"

Ash sang out his name, "Beeeeee-ckeeeeet."

He turned his head to look at me, confusion with a dash of anger on his face. "What the fuck?"

"Ash wanted to say hi," I said.

"What time is it?" he mumbled.

"Time to get up!" Ashley caroled. "It's a beautiful day! Why are you sleeping, anyway? Sleep is for quitters."

"She hasn't been to bed yet," I whispered.

With a sigh, Beckett propped himself up on his elbows, rubbing his eyes with both hands. I quickly shifted the camera back to my direction before Ashley could accidentally catch a glimpse of his wedding ring.

"Wait, put it back on Beck!" she protested.

"Why?"

"I have questions!" she said indignantly.

"Oh boy," he sighed.

"Hold on a sec…" I stretched out on my stomach beside Beckett, and turned the phone so we'd both fit on the screen.

"Ooh, hey!" Ash's expression brightened. "Both of you! So, Beckett, what's with the body, dude?"

"Huh?"

"You're, like, ripped. What gives? You seeing someone?"

Beckett scoffed. "Yeah, but she's 78. Oh, and dead." We'd been assigned to our cadavers for human anatomy class. Mine was a 63-year-old man. I giggled.

Ash made a gagging sound. "That's disgusting."

"No, it's gross." My joke was just for Beckett, since the class was called Gross Anatomy.

He laughed and held up a fist for me to bump.

Ash rolled her eyes, and changed the subject, asking what we'd been up to. Our answers were much less exciting than hers were when we asked her the same question. Ashley's life was filled with high-rollers, big spenders, men who gave her hundred dollar bills just for making them a limo reservation, or for getting them into a night club. She met celebrities, politicians, and people with more money than god. Beckett and I met…corpses and the other weirdos who were into cutting them open.

Hard to believe the three of us had been leading nearly identical lives just two months ago.

She tried, unsuccessfully, to get us to tell her anything interesting—the irony being that she would be completely transfixed by the news that we'd gotten married to pull off a long con on the University Housing department, but we were definitely *not* going to share that. So then she moved on to any interesting people we might have met.

"I really think you need to hook up with someone, Beck," Ash announced. "You were with Emily forever. It's time to get back out there."

"I don't have time," he tried.

"I'm not talking about a relationship. Just go out. Meet someone. Get some. You owe it to yourself."

His expression could not have been less impressed. "You woke me up for this?"

"Emmy, take him out!" Ash instructed me. "I'm putting you in charge of this. You know he'll never go alone."

I knew it was easiest to agree, so I did. Not long after that, Ashley started to run out of energy. She yawned, and declared it was time to go to sleep.

"That's exactly what we were doing," Beckett reminded her.

She yawned again. "Okay, well, I'm off to bed. Love you guys!"

"Love you, Ash," I said.

"Bye, Ash."

And then she disappeared from my screen. Beckett groaned. "I was really hoping to sleep in today."

"Me, too."

"You could have at least let me." He dropped his head onto the pillow. "I was having a good dream and everything."

"A sex dream?" I teased.

He just laughed.

"It was! Was it about me?"

"Fuck off."

"If it makes you feel any better, I have sex dreams about me, too."

"Shut up." He kicked my foot through the blankets.

"Seriously though, maybe we should go out. It's been non-stop school since we got here. You were already hard up before we left California. You're way overdue for rebound sex."

"I'm fine." He gave me a dirty look. "Besides, you haven't gotten any since we left California either."

"I can take care of myself, thank you very much."

"Oh really?" He flopped onto his side, giving me a once over.

"That's not what I—" Embarrassment clenched my chest, and I scowled at his smug expression. There was no way in hell I was going to let him win this. "So what if I do?"

He shrugged. "I'm not saying anything."

"You don't have to, I can read your mind. And you should be ashamed of yourself."

That made him laugh.

I stretched up into a cobra yoga pose, holding it for a second before hoisting myself to kneel beside him on the futon. It occurred to me that our little world had maybe gotten a bit too cozy if we could lie on the futon together without the excuse of a shared video call. A little too predictable. A little too…little. We really were turning into an old married couple with zero of the benefits. "We're going out tonight."

"Tonight?" His smugness was gone. "It's a Sunday."

"So?"

"So, we have class tomorrow morning."

"That never stopped us in undergrad."

"Yeah, but—"

"No buts. We're going out. Tonight."

15

THE WORLD'S WORST WINGMAN

*M*y plan was flawed from the start. We'd only been to one bar in town since we'd arrived, so I didn't know where the good places to go even were. I didn't want to ask anyone familiar with the area for suggestions, because I couldn't take the risk that they'd offer to show us around. There was no way I could get Beckett to meet someone if anyone who knew us as a married couple was with us.

I knew I was going to have to wing it. We wanted to be someplace within walking distance of the apartment so no one had to drive, and I knew where most of the stores, restaurants and bars were. We'd just head that direction and look for someplace with a crowd.

That evening, after a dinner of leftover pizza, I told Beckett to get dressed.

"You were serious about that?"

"One-hundred percent."

He made a face. "But I'm in my studying clothes." He was wearing a pair of navy blue UC-Irvine sweatpants and a cranberry-colored Middlesex hoodie.

"That's why you have to change." I was already dressed to go out in my favorite distressed jeans and a sweater. It wasn't exactly the kind of sexy I was used to, but it was Iowa and it was cold. I figured a covered up body was sexier than a frostbitten one.

After a bit more complaining, Beckett gave up and went into the bedroom to change. It only took him three minutes to come back out in jeans and a button-down shirt I hadn't seen since California. It must be so easy to be a guy. Not that he had a lot to choose from that was appropriate for cold weather. Neither of us did.

I have to confess that my eyes widened a bit at the new snug fit of the shirt across his expanded chest. Ashley hadn't been entirely off base with her whistling and catcalling. The gym agreed with Beckett. It agreed hard.

He held out his hands. "Satisfied?"

I blinked myself back into the here and now and nodded. "You'll do. Come on, let's go."

We put on our recently acquired heavy coats and went out into the dark evening. I still wasn't used to how much darker it was here at night. So much less light pollution. The stars looked crowded.

"All right, fearless leader, where are we going?" Beckett asked.

"This way," I said with a confidence I didn't feel. He couldn't know that I was bullshitting my way through this evening. I set off in the direction of downtown—such as it was. As we got closer, I realized I was getting excited. It really had been too long since I'd done anything fun. Anything irresponsible.

I smiled at Beckett. "This isn't so bad, is it?"

He shook his head, but he was smiling. "That remains to be seen."

It wasn't long before we hit River Street and the glow of bars open for business. There wasn't much action on the street, but it was a Sunday night, after all. We passed a couple of small bars that didn't appear to have more than a few diehard locals inside, and I acted like they weren't even there. Had to maintain the illusion that I had an actual plan. Then, though the plate glass and closed door of a larger outfit called Hawk's Sports Bar and Grille, we heard the sudden, loud, communal cheer that only comes from a group of people watching sports.

"Here we are," I announced, stopping in front of the door, and pointing through the glass. "Look, real live people."

"Whatever you say, boss."

We went inside just as the assembled people let out a collective groan.

"Bullshit!" someone shouted.

I looked at the TV and saw a crew of black-and-white-shirted officials conferring on a football field. Sunday Night Football. Green Bay Packers vs. Chicago Bears, and a quick glance around told me that this was a bar divided. So maybe this wasn't the best environment for finding Beckett a rebound girl, but I'd already acted like I meant to do this, so I had to fake it for a little while. I led him to the bar and found a place to squeeze in and order a couple of beers.

The bartender delivered and I turned my attention to surveying the place for prospects. That was when my second mistake hit home. Because I immediately saw a girl checking Beckett out. But as he raised his beer to take a drink, she saw the ring on his finger and looked away.

"Take your ring off," I whispered to him, already working off the one on my finger. How could I have been so stupid? Had I actually gotten used to the thing?

"Huh?" He wasn't listening. He was watching the action on the TVs.

Oh brother. We weren't going to get anywhere with him in a sports bar. He wasn't one of those nut-job sports fans, but he'd happily watch almost anything involving large men in uniform and a ball of any shape.

I leaned in to whisper in his ear. "Your ring. Take it off."

"Oh. Sure. Hold this." He handed me his beer and tried to get the ring off. Tried being the operative word, because after a minute of fussing, it was clear the silver band wasn't going anywhere. "Fuck," he muttered, shaking his hand. "It's really on there."

"What? How?"

"I don't know." His jaw clenched as he tried again. His ring finger was turning an angry red color. "Ow. Fuck it. It's not coming off."

"You have got to be kidding me!" I tried the ring myself, wiggling it back and forth until he pulled his hand away with a grunt.

"I'm not going to break my damn finger over this, Emmy."

I huffed in frustration. "Well this is going to make my job a lot fucking harder."

Beckett looked irritated for a second, but then he laughed. "You realize this is crazy, right? My *wife* is pissed off at me that I can't get my wedding ring off so she can hook me up with another girl."

I tried not to laugh, but he was right. It was completely absurd. I let out a snort, then fell into helpless laughter. "I guess we'll just have to find some girl who's into married guys."

He leaned in, his voice low in my ear. "They're going to think you're trying to get them into a threesome, you realize that, right?"

I had not realized that. I put a hand on his chest and pushed him back so I could see his eyes. "There are a lot of things I will do for you, Beck. But that is not one of them."

He grinned.

And that's when mistake number three became apparent.

"Beckett! Emmy!" a voice called from nearby.

I turned to find our classmate Reina beckoning us from a few feet away.

"Hey guys!" she called. "Come sit with us!"

What on earth had made me think we could go out in a town as small as River Glen and not run into a single person we knew? Although even if I'd thought of it, I wouldn't have expected to run into three of our fellow PA grad students hanging out in the exact bar we'd come to.

"We thought you were studying!" Reina said as she led us back to the table she was sharing with two other grad students, Travis and Keith, as well as two other people I didn't know.

"Hey guys!" Travis said.

Keith was transfixed by the TV, but he shot a glance and a wave at us. "Packers or Bears?" he asked.

"Uh…" I stammered. "Neither?"

"Cards," Beckett said, his tone indignant.

"Cardinals?" Travis said. "Please."

That was all it took to start a full-on football debate. A subject I couldn't care less about. I looked at Reina hopefully, but she was just as into it as the others. Turns out that Reina and Travis were both from the Chicago area and Keith was from Wisconsin. The other two with them—a woman named Jenny, and a man named Ron—were also originally from Wisconsin and Illinois, respectively. The five of them had decided to watch the game between the rival teams. It was pure coincidence that this was the night I'd declared to be our night on the town.

It was obvious in the first five minutes that we ran into them that there would be no wing-manning for me that night. The others weren't going to let us slip off now that they had found us. Plus the pitchers of beer kept reappearing, as well as baskets of freshly popped popcorn.

I had to admit, it wasn't the night I'd planned on, but it was still awfully nice to be out and doing something purely social. With the distraction of the game, none of the pathology students even talked about school. Which I'm sure Jenny and Ron appreciated, even if they didn't know it.

"So how'd you two meet?" Jenny asked me at a commercial break.

"We met in our first biology class in undergrad."

"College sweethearts," she said in a singsong voice, smiling.

I just laughed.

"Don't worry, they're not one of *those* couples," Reina said. I must have looked confused, because she explained. "You guys are very chill. You're not all over each other, and 'I love you, honey bunny!' all the time."

Imagine that, I thought, giving Beckett a look from the corner of my eyes. He'd overheard the comment and slung his arm around my shoulders. "How did you guess my little nickname for Emmy?" He looked at me, grinning, "Did you tell them, honey bunny?"

"Aww, I'm sorry, schmoopy, was that supposed to be a secret?" I teased.

Reina laughed. "See? That's exactly what I mean. You remind me of my brother and his wife. They've been together forever, so they're not in the obnoxious horny stage anymore."

"Easy not to be obnoxious when you know you can get some whenever you want," Ron said. Then he seemed to realize what he'd said and gave me a sheepish smile. "I mean, if you're both into it."

Jenny laughed. "Ooh, I dig that sexy mutual consent talk."

"You know me. Enlightened, twenty-first century man."

The game came back on, and with only two minutes left in the fourth quarter, everyone's attention was glued to the screens. The Packers won, with mixed reactions from the bar's patrons, and our table. It was easy for me, since I could traitorously cheer for both sides. There was a bit of sulking from the Chicago fans, but then the TVs turned back to a variety of other sports and analysis of the game under closed captioning, and the bartender turned up the music instead.

We spent the rest of the night working our way through a few more pitchers and having normal, non-pathology related conversations. It was a nice change. Beckett and I ended up telling a few stories of our time in undergrad. I was amazed by how easy it was to pretend we'd been a couple all those years. There wasn't much difference between dating someone and living with them, except of course for the sex, but it wasn't like we'd be telling those stories anyway.

At midnight, Reina declared that we should all get to bed if we were going to survive a full day of classes on Monday, and everyone agreed to pack it in. Ron offered to give us a ride home, but I didn't think he had any business behind the wheel, much less with me in the car. Jenny convinced him to Uber it home, while Beckett and I walked.

Somehow it had gotten even colder and I slid my arm through Beckett's, clinging to him for warmth as we walked. Half a dozen beers had my brain on spin cycle and my feet clumsy.

"So, I completely failed you," I said.

"It's okay," he said. "I actually had fun. Ashley was right, I needed to get out." His voice had a familiar, thick sound that I recognized from nights out at the bars in Irvine.

"She didn't say get out, she said get some."

"Eh." He shrugged.

I shivered and snuggled closer to him. God, it was cold. "Aren't you…lonely? You were with Emily for so long."

"We didn't live in the same state. I'm used to long dry spells." He sighed. "Really. Long. Dry spells."

"I don't just mean that. You talked to her on the phone all the time. Do you miss that? The relationship part?"

"Sometimes. Things weren't exactly great over the summer."

"Oh. I didn't…"

"I just figured it would be better after we were together."

"That's a big gamble, Beck."

"Yeah. I see that. Now."

"I'm sorry. I didn't know."

"I didn't tell you."

We turned the final corner to our block, and the sight of our building made me happy. It was starting to feel something like home.

He let out a soft, sad laugh. "To be honest, you're a better girl-friend than she was at the end."

"I'm not your girrrfriend. Girlfriend," I corrected automatically, my slurred word blunting my indignation.

"That's my point."

"Ouch."

"Yeah."

We walked in silence until we got to the outside door of Overlook, and I stood shivering while Beckett let us in with his key. I scrambled in behind him and gave a full body shake.

"I'm f-f-f-f-reezing!"

He laughed, rubbing his hands up and down my arms. "I hate to tell you, but I'm pretty sure it gets colder than this."

I shook my head. "No. I reject that."

He laughed again, and took one of my hands between his, rubbing life into my numb fingers.

"Uhhh," I moaned happily, giving him my other hand. "See? You're a good husband. You deserve a wife who can get you laid."

"Stop," he said. "I'm fine. You're obsessing. Come on." He tugged my elbow until I followed him to the second floor, where I slumped against the wall beside the door while Beckett fumbled with the key.

"Don't you miss sex?" I confessed, "I miss sex."

Beckett dropped his keys.

I giggled, and put my foot over them when he bent to pick them up.

"Move." He smacked my ankle, laughing, but I didn't move. He snagged the edge of one of the jump rings and yanked the keys free, making me lose my balance. I caught myself on the door frame as Beckett got to his feet. "You're a pain in the ass, you know that?" he said.

"Answer the question."

Beckett ignored me, looking around me to fit his key in the lock. It clicked softly as he unlocked it, but I put my hand on his wrist. "You okay?" I asked.

He stopped trying to open the door and looked in my eyes for a long moment. "Can I tell you something?"

My breath caught. "Yes."

"I...I don't actually miss it that much."

"Really?"

"It's not that much different than what I can do...alone, you know?"

It was perhaps the saddest thing I'd ever heard. Still, I tried to meet him halfway. "I mean, sure, the end result is basically the same, but what about all the other stuff?"

He nodded, like I should continue.

"The kissing, and the naked bodies, and the touching, and just that...you know, that *thing*."

"I guess..."

"Do you know what I mean?"

"Um..."

I couldn't think how to explain, so I slid my hands around his hips, pulling him to me. Our bodies were lined up from knees to chest, and even with our heavy coats on I could feel the weight and heat of him. I closed my eyes, and tilted my face up to his, not kissing him, not wanting him to kiss me. Just grazing my cheek against his, and breathing the same air for a moment. This was the intangible *thing* I meant. The closeness, the electricity between two people.

"This," I whispered. "Don't you miss the spark?"

His fingertips grazed my jaw and my throat, and his nose nuzzled mine.

"Emmy," he breathed.

I closed my eyes again, this time wanting to be kissed. Wanting to see if this spark could build a fire.

But a door clicked open down the hall, and we jumped.

My pulse rushed in my ears as Beckett straightened up, away from me.

"We should go inside," he said.

"Right."

He stood back while I opened the door, and said, "You can use the bathroom first," as soon as we were inside.

I guessed that meant the conversation was over. And maybe I'd been the only one feeling electricity after all. Electricity I had no right to feel.

Go to bed, Emmy, I thought. *Before you do something stupid.*

16

LITTLE ORPHAN EMMY

*M*y dad and I had a standing date on the phone every Monday night. With him traveling all over the country, it gave me a little sense of security to know that he'd check in once a week. Often the calls were short. Just a check-in. *How are things? How's school? Do you need anything? Where are you now? Where are you going next? Feeling okay? Are you going to settle down somewhere soon?*

I worried about him. I knew the cross-country traveling had always been his dream retirement, but he was supposed to be in an RV with my mom. Not flying solo on a motorcycle. It was his grieving process when he got started. I never expected it to last almost four years.

Now that it was November, I knew he'd be in the South somewhere. That was the beauty of being mobile. He followed good weather wherever he wanted to go. And I knew from personal experience, that did not mean up where I was these days. Beckett had been right—it could get colder. In fact, it could snow. I'd never seen snow in real life before that wasn't on a mountain. It was gorgeous. And it sucked.

The week before Thanksgiving, I happily answered the phone to my dad's call.

"So, baby girl, I've got some news," he said.

"What's up?"

"I, uh, I'm in Canada."

"Canada?" I was stunned. Talk about cold. "What are you doing up there?"

"Well, see, that's the thing. I've sort of…met someone."

Oh. I'd known this could happen. In some ways I'd hoped it would. But hearing it out loud felt like having a bucket of cold water dumped over my head. "You did?"

"Yeah. She's a wonderful lady. I think you're going to like her."

I forced my throat to open. "That's great, daddy." Damn that quaver.

"Anyway, she's invited me to Thanksgiving with her son and his family."

"Isn't Canadian Thanksgiving in October?" Way to focus on the important issues here, Em. Why the heck did I even know that?

"It is," he said, sounding surprised. "But, uh, Charlene's family lives in Alaska, so…regular Thanksgiving."

"Alaska?" I repeated. "How far north are you?"

"I'm in the Yukon Territory. Near Whitehorse."

My mind tried to call up a map of Canada, but apart from a rough idea of Vancouver and Toronto, it might as well say "Here Be Monsters." Still, I knew Yukon Territory was north. Very north. "Oh, wow."

"I know I should have told you about this sooner, but I just wasn't sure how to bring it up."

Not sure how to bring it up? I thought. *Maybe try saying anything. Anything at all. Any words. Give me a single clue that you'd even spoken to a woman?* "So, um, what are you saying?"

"Well, I'd love for you to come up to Alaska and join us for Thanksgiving. Charlene's son said to invite you."

"Dad, I'm, uh..."

"I looked into some flights and, well, they're a bit on the expensive side."

"I bet." Not to mention long. I'd spend more time on a plane than with my dad.

"So, if you wanted to do something else for Thanksgiving this year, I would understand."

I told myself that he was trying to be understanding. But it felt a bit like he was telling me not to come. A tiny voice inside me insisted that couldn't be true, but it was hard to hear over the roaring noise of the crowd in my head shouting that he didn't want me to come.

"Um, yeah," I stammered. "I'll probably just do that. I've gotten a few invites already."

"You have? Oh that's good to hear." He sounded relieved.

"Dad, I'm sorry, I gotta go. But we'll talk soon, okay?" My voice was rising to cartoon squeakiness. I had to get off the phone, STAT.

"Okay, baby girl. I love you so much."

"Love you too, dad. Bye." I hung up before he could say anything else and tossed the phone down like it bit me. My stiff fingers seemed determined to search my face for the mythical No Crying switch, pressing the bridge of my nose, and my cheek bones, fanning my face. But it was all pointless. I was going to cry and there was nothing to stop me.

Which is exactly what I was still doing when Beckett came into the bedroom.

"Wha—I didn't know you were in—whoa. What's wrong?"

I told him between hiccuping sounds, and disgusting, hard sniffles. I didn't have to get very far into it before he was sitting next to me, his arm around my shoulders and consoling me.

"I'm sure he'd be happy if you came, Emmy," he said. And, "Of course he wants to see you." And, "You should go if you want to go."

"But I don't want to!" I wailed. "I don't want to fly to Alaska for, what? Two days? I don't want to spend Thanksgiving with some strangers I've never met before!"

He didn't say anything, just squeezed my shoulders.

"I've seen those TV shows," I went on miserably. "What if they're like those bush people? What if they live off the grid and have an outhouse? I don't want to spend Thanksgiving in an outhouse!"

He was trying valiantly not to laugh, but the shaking of his shoulders gave him away. I elbowed him in the stomach. "It's not funny!"

"Em, they wouldn't make you spend Thanksgiving in the outhouse."

"You don't know that!" I sniffled, but a choked laugh escaped me. "How did he even meet someone from Alaska? And what is he doing in Canada in November? It must be horrible."

Beckett pressed his hand against my head until I let it rest on his shoulder, then gave me a gentle kiss on the hair. "I'm sorry."

The sigh that escaped me was the kind that deflates you like a balloon. I sagged further into Beckett, slithering one arm around his waist for comfort. "Why can't he just be in San Jose like a normal dad? Why can't I just have a house to go home to?"

"I don't know." Beckett didn't say anything more for a long time, just holding me and patting me gently on the arm. "I'm kind of jealous, to be honest. I don't want to go home for Thanksgiving."

"You don't?"

"They're all going to want to talk about Emily."

"And you don't."

"I do not."

I sniffled, and tried not to let my nose run onto his shirt. "Can I make an observation?"

"What?"

"You don't really seem to ever want to talk about Emily."

"I don't."

"Do you think that's healthy?"

"Are you advocating for irrational breakdowns about outhouses instead?"

I laughed and gave him a gentle shove with my shoulder. "Don't question my methods."

Beckett sighed, slouching a bit. "I don't feel like there's anything to say. She completely fucked over my life. Nobody can say anything to change that. And now...I don't even know if we were ever right in the first place."

"Why do you say that?"

"My first hint was that she was planning to leave me at the altar for months. It was a pretty good clue that maybe we weren't meant to be."

I cringed at his acidic tone. "Right."

"But also...I don't really miss her that much. Which is a fucking insane thing to say about someone you were planning to marry."

"It's not great," I had to admit.

He let his arm drop from my shoulders, but it stayed planted on the bed behind me. "And maybe there wasn't a spark, and I just never knew it."

My mind flashed on the drunken moment in the hallway when I decided to show him spark. The way his fingertips had trailed down my cheek, the place he never touched when we were playing husband and wife. "There must have been at some point," I tried. "When you first met."

"Maybe." He rubbed his eyes. "But I was sixteen and she seemed interested. That was enough then."

I wanted to protest. To be able to assure him that he hadn't wasted his time with her, but he was making it hard. And I didn't want to interrupt. Now that the guy who didn't want to talk about her was talking about her, maybe it was for the best just to let him go.

"God, I think waiting was half of it. Only so far and then, nope. She was saving herself. That fucking purity ring. It drove me crazy. I just wanted her to say yes."

This was news to me. I had no idea that Emily had taken one of those purity vows. "But she did, right?"

"Yep. Three years, two months, and twenty-six days later. But who's fucking counting, right? Winter break, sophomore year. She cried. Told me now we had to get married or she was going to hell. Exactly what you want for your first time, right?"

Holy. Shit. I could not believe what I was hearing. "Oh my god, Beckett that sounds awful."

"Yeah, well…" he shrugged. "There's a reason I don't really talk about it."

"I never would have thought—she seemed pretty normal the couple times I met her. And her letter—there was nothing about hell."

"Yeah, I noticed that. She's been less…Jesus-y for the last year. I figured being away from her parents had something to do with it."

The idea formed in my mind, complete and sure. She'd met someone else. I was certain of it even though I had no proof. No reason. It just made sense to me. People so rarely changed their fundamental beliefs for no reason. I wanted to tell him, but I knew it would only hurt him. I bit my cheek and kept my own counsel.

Suddenly Beckett straightened up. "You know what? Fuck it. I'm not going home. I don't want to, and you don't need to be alone on Thanksgiving."

"I won't be alone," I said. "Reina already asked if we wanted to go to her family's Thanksgiving. So did Keith. So did Ginny and Tom. I'll be fine."

"And how will you explain why you're not going with your husband for the holiday?"

"Uhh…"

"You won't." He put his arm back around my shoulders and gave me a squeeze. "I'm not leaving you, Mrs. Anderson."

"I'm not an Anderson."

"We can't all be perfect."

17

OVER OUR HEADS

*W*e accepted Reina's invitation to join her family for Thanksgiving. It was a good deal for her too, since we gave her a ride. She was from Schaumburg, just outside Chicago, which turned out to be basically a well-developed suburb. Big box stores, hotels, and wide, busy streets. Her family lived in a nice neighborhood on a cul-de-sac where there were already holiday lights on most of the houses, and interior lights glowing from the windows.

Reina had warned us on the way over that her mom, Claudia, would hug us, which she did, and that she would immediately offer us something to eat, which she did. But it was after nine, and the three of us had done a fast food on the road dinner.

"Go on down and tell dad you're here. Your brothers are already here."

Reina beckoned for us to follow her and we went down a set of stairs to a family room. She introduced us to her father, her older brother Oscar and his wife Julia, and her younger brother Thomas.

"Oh thank god, females!" Julia said, leaping up to hug Reina and then me. I was startled, but I let her. They were obviously a hugging family. "I keep telling your mom to stop working, or let me help, but you know."

"Of course."

Reina's dad, who insisted we called him Pete, offered drinks and went behind a well-equipped home bar in the corner to get us anything we asked for. I felt like I'd walked into a movie about the 1950s. Even before my mom died, I was an only child, and my family had never really been the conventional type. My parents both worked long hours in Silicon Valley, and I spent a lot of time at daycare, and at after school programs. My mom was a terrible cook, so Thanksgiving dinner was usually ordered from the local deli. It wasn't a movie-perfect life, but it was my life, and it's what I was used to. This all felt a bit unreal to me.

Within minutes, we had drinks and Reina gave everyone a bit of background on us. I still hadn't gotten used to hearing the lies about us from other people's mouths. Guilt never failed to knot up in my chest when I thought about what we had done. Even if we were legally married. Even if we really had met in our freshman year biology class. Even if we'd been roommates and friends all the years we claimed to be. It had never been love at first sight. There had always been the other Emily. The real Emily.

But of course, I played along, and turned the conversation back to them as quickly as I could without seeming shady. I liked Pete, Oscar, Julia, and Thomas. They were fun, and funny, and it was obvious they liked each other. Not the kind of family that got together on holidays just to bitch at each other. Just the opposite in fact. They seemed thrilled to be in the same room, and soon enough we were being taught the rules of a card game called Knock. It was really simple, but there was a lot of chance involved and plenty of opportunity to smack talk, which Reina's family seemed to be professionals at. A few hands in, her mom joined us, and the ribbing got even more intense.

Just by chance, I got on a winning streak, and Pete decided the only solution was to make it harder for me to do math, so he poured me a strong drink. Vodka soda, since I told him I couldn't handle the whiskey he offered. And the gambit paid off, as my math skills declined with each sip.

I didn't realize how long we'd been playing until Reina's mom declared that she had to get to bed if the turkey was going to be properly cooked the next day. The rest of us lasted through a few more rounds, but then Julia started yawning, and I couldn't resist the contagion, covering my wide mouth with my last hand of cards.

"Why don't I show you guys your room?" Reina said with a smile.

It hadn't occurred to me until that moment that Beckett and I would be sharing a room. Which was idiotic of me, considering Reina thought we were married. We *were* married, for heaven's sake. Of course we'd be in the same room.

She took us back to the entry to get our bags, then led us into a small room that was obviously an office most of the time, and I wanted to kick myself. Not just the same room, the same bed. Duh.

"Sorry it's not much. With my brothers both here, you guys are stuck on the fold out couch."

"It's fine," I said cheerfully. "This is great, thanks."

"On the plus side, you don't have to share a bathroom with anyone." She pointed to the door across the hall. "It's even got a shower."

"Great." Beckett sounded as cheerful as I did. In other words, Fakey McFalsecheer. "Thanks again for having us, Reina."

"I'm happy you guys came." She told us to help ourselves to anything in the fridge and said we should sleep in. After triple checking that we didn't need anything, she excused herself to her own room, leaving us standing in the tiny space at the foot of the fold out couch. The bed was already set up and made up nicely with extra blankets draped over the arms of the couch and plenty of pillows. It was all very homey and inviting.

And small.

I looked at Beckett. "Well…"

"I can go sleep on the couch," he offered.

"Don't be ridiculous. How would we explain that?" I propped my hands on my hips. "This will be fine."

"Are you sure?"

"Come on, Beck, we've shared a room before."

"True." He sounded doubtful.

"Just don't snore and we'll be fine." I elbowed him, then dropped my duffle bag on the end of the bed to dig out some pajamas. The bathroom made it easy to change in private. It wasn't much different than being in our apartment at home. And after two and a half years of being roommates, we'd probably seen more of each other in our pajamas than in regular clothes by this point.

After a brief crawl under the desk to find a plug for my phone cable, I got in bed, sorting through the pillow offerings to find one I liked while Beckett was in the bathroom. Every move drew metallic squeaks from the frame, but if I lay perfectly still, it was quiet. I made sure I was as motionless as a statue under the blankets when Beckett returned so he could experience the noisiness for himself.

He seemed to be playing it cool just like I was doing, and he didn't say anything as he looked for an outlet on his side of the bed and then lifted covers. The frame creaked beneath his weight, and I tried not to laugh when he froze in surprise. Hard to put on that calm, cool, and collected front when the furniture was announcing our every breath. The fold out was too narrow to ignore each other; our elbows bumped as soon as Beckett lay down. A giggle bubbled up in my throat, but I pressed my lips together and tried to pull my elbow tight against my side to give him an extra inch. But he kept wiggling and shifting the blankets while the frame played a discordant symphony, until his last move uncovered my entire right half.

"Hey!" I protested, grabbing the edge before he could take it all.

"Oh, sorry." He wafted the blankets up to recover me, but he didn't stop shifting and wiggling, and the bed didn't stop screeching.

The giggle escaped me. "What are you doing?!"

"There's a spring..." He sat up and poked his thumb into a spot on the mattress. The frame groaned and popped.

"Shhh, you're making it mad," I whispered, giggling.

"Trade places with me," he said.

"Hell no! Why should I have to have the spring in my back?"

"You're way lighter than me, you won't even feel it."

"No way!"

"Come on, please?"

"Nope. I got in bed first. I got the good spot fair and square."

"Emmy, please? Can you just check if you feel it?"

"Oh, fine!" I said, tossing the blankets back. I crawled across the top of the bed, while Beckett shuffled across the bottom, his weight making the spring groan and pop so loudly I worried he was going to fall through.

In his former spot, I wiggled into position. The spring was slightly noticeable, but if I scooted just a bit to the right, I could avoid it.

"Well?" he prompted.

"Fine. You can have the other side," I said. "But if you don't like that side, I'm not switching back."

He tried my spot, and deemed it acceptable. "Can you maybe move a little bit that way?" His elbow nudged mine.

"That's where the spring is."

"Fine." He sighed.

I sat up briefly to turn off the lamp on my side of the bed and then we were in the dark together. In the immediate disorientation of no light, I felt suddenly much closer to Beckett than I had been just a second before. And even though I'd flopped down on the bed and the futon in our apartment beside him, even though he'd once shared his blankets with me for a few minutes in a cold motel in western Iowa, we'd never gone to bed together intentionally before. I was so aware of him. The slightest movement of his arm or leg transmitted to me. I hadn't slept beside anyone since Ashley passed out in my bed in Irvine.

"Reina's family seems really nice," I said when the quiet got to be too awkward to bear.

"They do."

"I feel kind of bad that we're lying to them."

He went perfectly still. "It's not technically lying."

"Beckett, come on."

"I know."

"I didn't really think this part through."

"What part?" he asked.

"I knew we wouldn't tell our current friends or our families. And I feel bad about that, but I didn't think about the new people we'd meet. Ginny and Tom, and everyone else in Overlook, and Reina, and Jon, and Keith, and Mandy, and Travis…all the PA students. All our professors. They all believe us."

"Yeah," he said.

"It's just…it's going to be a lot harder than I thought to end this."

He was quiet for a long time, though I was certain he hadn't fallen asleep. There was too much tension in his body. Finally he spoke. "You're right. I don't know. It's going to be…awkward."

I hadn't put words to any of these fears before, and now that I had, my mind was reeling with the consequences and possible solutions. "Maybe we could get an apartment off campus next year. Just stay roommates. We'll get the annulment and we just won't tell anyone."

Beckett let out a soft, ironic laugh. "So there will be the people we never tell we got married, and the people we never tell we got un-married. That won't be weird at all."

"Relationship status: it's complicated." As it was, we'd both agreed to ramp down our social media lives. All we needed was a new friend to make some comment that would tip off our old friends.

He sighed. "We'll figure something out."

"I guess we could just break up." For some reason, the idea made my stomach hurt.

"We'll figure it out," he said firmly, as if that weren't an option.

18

DO YOU LIKE TEARS ON YOUR TURKEY?

*W*hen I woke up in the morning, I was definitely hogging the bed. The spring to my left had driven me toward the middle already, but I seemed to have done the rest of the job while I was sleeping. I was now curled on my side, tucked right up behind Beckett like a little spoon. Except I also had my hands under my chin, which put my elbows in his back. I'd moved so close, my head was on his pillow.

Whoops.

I tried to ease my way back to my side without him noticing, but of course the creaking springs betrayed me before I could get even an inch away.

"Oh, now you move?" Beckett said in a low voice, thick with sleep.

"Sorry," I mumbled. As I scooted back to my side of the bed, I found the sheets cold, which meant I hadn't been over there in a while.

"S'okay," he said. "At least you didn't steal all the blankets. Emily used to do that."

It was the first time I'd heard him volunteer anything about her in a while. "She did?"

"Mmm-hmm." He rolled onto his back, grabbed the blankets tight and rolled away from me again, taking all the covers with him.

"Hey!"

"Like that."

I seized the edge of the blanket and pulled hard until he rolled to his back again, giving me about a foot of coverage. "Well, then you're lucky you didn't marry her."

"Yeah, everything else was perfect. The blanket was the deal-breaker for sure."

I checked to be sure he was joking before I laughed, but then we were both laughing. And you know how sometimes you get one of those thoughts? Those images that pop into your mind so perfectly clear that they might as well be reality. Like standing on a station platform and imagining jumping in front of it? Except this time I saw myself rolling toward Beckett and kissing him. As though it wouldn't shock him. As if he might cup my neck and pull me closer and kiss me back.

I blinked, hard, and scooted the rest of the way to my side of the bed, mindless of the rogue spring as it poked me in the ribs when I sat up. Pretending the groaning springs weren't giving away my hurry. I needed to get up, and be with other people right now. Have normal thoughts.

∼

REINA'S FAMILY made us as welcome on the actual holiday as they had the night before. I sipped coffee and watched the Macy's Thanksgiving Day Parade on a small TV on the kitchen table while Reina and her mom put out a spread of baked French toast and bacon. Her dad told me the family theory that you had to eat a big breakfast on Thanksgiving if you were going to manage to stuff yourself at dinner. "You gotta get your stomach warmed up," Pete told me.

I watched from the breakfast bar while Claudia, Reina, and Julia got to work on the side dishes. The turkey was getting ready to meet its fate in a huge deep fryer out in the yard. That seemed to be the domain of Pete, Oscar, and Thomas, with special guest supervisor Beckett. The clichéd division of labor among the men and women made me smile, even while I was mentally rolling my eyes a bit. It was clear that they were all falling into roles they'd had all their lives, though, and no one complained. I offered to help, with the warning that my skills in the kitchen were in the Ramen noodles and Lean Cuisine area. The women decided I could be trusted to open cans for green bean casserole.

When Claudia realized I hadn't been exaggerating my lack of skills, she took extra time to talk me through the rest of the recipe. Honestly, it's a dish a five-year-old could handle, but I was absurdly proud of the casserole dish when it was all prepped and ready for the oven. I'd have to make sure to tell Beckett it was my handiwork later.

"Your mother doesn't want you to help her when she's in the kitchen?" Claudia asked me when she saw me staring transfixed while she stirred some flour into melted butter. Her smile was kind.

"I got my cooking skills directly from her," I said. "I'm not even sure she knew how to work the stove."

Reina looked at me in alarm. "Mom, Emmy's mom died a few years ago."

Claudia gave me The Look. The mixture of sympathy and horror and curiosity and shame. I'd seen it hundreds of times since my mom died. I wished it could be overdone to the point of being painless. But it still managed to trigger the crying reflex in my brain. "I'm so sorry," she whispered. "I didn't know."

I forced a smile. "It's okay."

"How did it happen?" she asked.

"Car accident," I said, and then because everyone wanted to

know, even if they wouldn't admit it, I added, "She was killed instantly. She didn't suffer."

"Oh dear god." Claudia wiped her hands on a towel and gave me a tight hug. "You poor girl."

And just what was I supposed to do then besides burst into tears? It wasn't my fault. I was powerless. She was warm and kind and a mom. I am not made of stone.

I buried my face in her shoulder and sobbed, wishing like hell that I could stop. It was so embarrassing. I didn't know these people. They didn't deserve to have me crying all over their nice family holiday. Fuck.

But Claudia just patted my back and stroked her hand over my hair and didn't show any sign of letting me go. She just said things like, "That's all right. Let it out."

After god knew how long, I felt a new, cold hand on my back, and then Claudia was transferring me to Beckett's arms. He held me in a tight hug, rocking me.

"It's okay, baby, I've got you," he said softly.

I stayed there for a long time, until the worst of the crying ended with my sinuses and throat aching, and my eyes hot and swollen. When I finally felt like I could talk again, I said, "I'm sorry, you guys."

"Don't be." Beckett planted a kiss on top of my head. "There's nothing to be sorry for."

"Emmy," Reina said my name like a complete sentence and put her arms around both Beckett and me.

"I, for one, am glad we can have you with us." Claudia joined the group hug.

"Well don't leave me out!" Julia declared, glomming on to the bundle of humans in the kitchen.

I laughed, a thick, post-crying laugh, and tilted my head back to get some air. It's not easy being the shortest person in the middle of a group hug. Beckett looked down at me and made a face that seemed to say, "Well, what can you do?"

"When in Rome…" I said to him.

He smiled and touched the tip of his nose to mine. It was about all he could manage in the pile-on, but it set off a warmth that spread through me.

Finally the hug broke up. Claudia put her warm hand on my shoulder. "Now, would you like to put your feet up for a while? Or would you like to learn a little more about the kitchen?"

"I'll stay if that's okay with you."

"You bet."

~

GOOGLE TOLD me it was three hours earlier in Alaska, so I didn't talk to my dad until the early afternoon. He sounded so happy when I called, it almost made me start crying again. We chatted for a few minutes, and he told me he wished I'd been able to make it, but he understood why I didn't want to fly all the way to Alaska.

"How did you even meet someone in Alaska, dad?"

"She lives in Canada. But we met online."

The image of my father on Tinder swept into my head, but I rejected it immediately. There was no way in hell. "Oh, that's uh…"

"It's a group for people who've lost a spouse."

"Oh." I never knew what to say about my mom. I'd been home for the summer when she died, but I hadn't gone back to San Jose since. I knew my dad was alone up there. I knew he had to be hurting as much as I was. But we'd both agreed that I should go back to school when the fall came around. Since then, we just didn't really talk about her much at all. He'd said she'd be proud of me when I graduated.

Perhaps I needed to deal with her death a bit more, if sobbing all over Reina's mom was any indication.

I couldn't fix it all right then. I didn't want to end up crying on the phone. But maybe I could do one thing. "I hope you have a great day, dad," I said. "I miss you."

"I miss you too, baby girl."

"Love you."

"Love you more."

I got off the phone quickly for fear of a repeat of the morning's tear fest, but I felt a little better. Slightly less resentful that my dad was spending Thanksgiving with someone else's family.

~

EVERYONE CALLED it an early night that night. There was just no fighting the turkey. It had been hours since I'd taken a single bite of food and I was still stuffed. Beckett and I took turns in the bathroom again and I didn't bother trying to get the good side of the bed. I knew he'd make the same arguments about our relative weights. Besides, I now knew I'd just make myself comfortable on his side if the spring bothered me. Take that, Beckett.

He returned from the bathroom and didn't say anything until he was under the covers. Then he karate chopped the mattress between us and said, "This is your dance space. This is my dance space."

I burst out laughing. "Now all I want to do is come over there. Lay right on top of you, maybe."

He groaned and put a blocking elbow out a few inches. "Don't touch me. I might explode," he said.

"Me, too." I leaned over to turn out the light, then positioned myself as comfortably as I could without invading his territory. There was a little space between us, but it wasn't like I could avoid him completely on the narrow fold out.

"I don't think I've ever eaten that much food in my life," Beckett moaned.

"Seriously. That was nothing like my version of Thanksgiving."

"Mine either." He paused. "Everyone was too happy."

"Are you sorry you didn't go home?"

"Not at all." Our hands were flopped lifelessly on the mattress between us, and now he slid his over to softly squeeze my fingers.

I wasn't sorry either, and when he started to pull his hand away, I caught two of his fingers with my thumb. "Thank you."

"For what?"

"For this morning. And last week. For deciding not to go back to Arizona. Just for being there for me."

"Always." His fingers curled tighter around my thumb for a second.

But it wouldn't be always. It wouldn't even be much longer. And in a lot of ways, I was going to miss this ridiculous sham. "Of all my fake husbands, you're probably the best," I said.

He laughed, and stroked one finger along the side of my thumb. "You're in my top ten wives, for sure."

"Claudia and Pete already invited us back for next year. Would it be weird to stay married just for her pumpkin pie?"

"People have stayed married for worse reasons."

"Than pie?"

"For sure. I'm pretty sure my parents are only married because they don't want the other one to get the house in a divorce."

"Ouch." At least my parents had been happy together.

"Yeah. It's pretty great."

His wedding band was positioned against my thumb, and I began to play with it, rotating it around his finger, sliding it the little bit that it would move up and down. "If Emily's parents hadn't been so uptight about you living together, would you have wanted to get married?" I thought I knew the answer, but I'd never asked so directly.

"No," he said softly. "Not yet."

"So...?" I prompted.

"I loved her. At least I thought I did." He flicked his finger to free his ring from my exploring fingers, and I expected his hand to disappear entirely. Instead he matched his fingertips to mine and spread them wide so we were palm-to-palm, like reflections in a mirror. "Maybe I didn't." His fingers shifted just a hair to the left, weaving between mine.

My heart was tripping over nerves. At the dangerous territory of this conversation, or the unexpected intimacy of his thumb rubbing circles on my skin? I didn't know. "I'm glad you didn't marry her."

"I bet." I could hear the laughter in his voice, though he was invisible to me in the dark. "You'd be homeless."

"Well, okay, yes. But that's not what I meant." I bit my lip. "I think you wouldn't have been happy. And I want you to be happy."

He didn't say anything for a moment, though his thumb continued to draw circles on me. "I'm happy, Em."

"Good."

"I think you might actually be in the top five of my favorite wives."

"A promotion!" I teased. "Does that come with a raise?"

"No. But you'll get a nice certificate to hang in your cubicle."

"Wow."

"You're welcome."

We both went quiet then, and I wondered if I should take my hand away. But the truth was, I didn't want to. It had been an emotional day, and there was something so comforting about the warm touch of his skin against mine. It was a wonder I could hunger for human contact with the amount of time Beckett and I spent playing Affectionate Newlyweds. But none of that was real. This was real. At least, I thought it was. And it had been so long since I'd had something real. I wasn't going to be the one who let go.

So instead I fell asleep with his hand clasped in mine.

19

POSTCARDS FROM THE
SUBCONSCIOUS

*T*he first dream came a few nights after we got home from Reina's house. Thank god I was alone, because I woke up panting and arching my back, my hands curled into fists full of blankets. I would have had to play it off as a nightmare if it had happened over Thanksgiving weekend.

Under normal circumstances, I would think having a sex dream about your husband would be a good sign. You're clearly still into him. Things are good. He's the guy for you. But I was not only not into Beckett, I was on my way to getting an annulment from him on the grounds of non-consummation. We'd come into this marriage completely platonic and it was pure lunacy for my subconscious to start getting crazy ideas about him now.

It was okay, I told myself. Nothing to panic about. I'd had sexy dreams about friends before. It didn't mean anything. I'd had dreams about strangers in coffee shops, celebrities I'd only seen on TV, male, female...didn't matter. It was just my subconscious cleaning house. Tossing together image salad with a bit of unfulfilled sexual need dressing.

That's probably all this dream was, I coached myself. I was on a severe sex diet. Beckett was the person I saw most often. And our little husband and wife charade meant that I knew what his hands felt like on my waist, and what he looked like without a shirt, and what his mouth tasted like. The real surprise was that it had never happened before, right?

Without warning, images from the dream burst in my head like fireworks. Beckett wrapping his arms around me from behind and dragging his tongue up my neck. Beckett tugging my shirt over my head and cupping my breasts. Beckett smiling up at me with the elastic of my panties in his teeth. Beckett on top of me. Beckett inside me.

I crossed my legs, squeezing my thighs together. Fuck. This was way more than my usual sex dream. Most of those ended in the make-out stage. Left me feeling a little buzzed. A little randy.

This one had me twisted in knots. My fingertips tingled and my breath came in shallow gasps. I had a feeling I'd only been seconds from finishing when I woke up.

Fuck.

The bedroom door clicked open and I slammed my eyes shut, feigning sleep. Beckett's footsteps followed the short path from bedroom to bathroom. When I heard the other door close, I rolled onto my stomach, staring in the direction of the bathroom. Did he know I was faking sleep? Did he somehow sense what was in my head from behind the closed door and come out here just so I'd know he knew?

The shower turned on. Thank god. I needed some clean underwear, STAT.

I hurried out of bed and ran into the bedroom, closing the door behind me. He never took long in the shower, so I would only have a few minutes to make sure he wouldn't come in to find me half-dressed with damp underwear clutched in one hand. Talk about awkward.

I changed quickly and buried my panties deep in my hamper. Hiding the evidence. Like he was going to come in here and immediately notice my dirty clothes. Like there wasn't another pair of underpants sitting in full view at the top the hamper from yesterday. I churned the whole pile to make sure there was nothing lacy, silky, or strappy visible, then hurried out of the room.

Back in the living room, I eyeballed the scrambled sheets on the futon with suspicion. Was there some kind of invisible sign there? If he sprayed the room with a mysterious psychic Luminol, would it broadcast my secret? *Emmy had a sex dream about you last night!*

I had to get a hold of myself. This was ridiculous. So I forced myself to walk calmly to the coffee machine and press the power button.

There we go. Normal stuff. Everything was fine. I could make coffee and fold my sheets up for the day. I could throw a bagel in the toaster. I was the very picture of normalcy.

When Beckett emerged from the bathroom with a towel wrapped around his hips, I was leaning casually against the kitchen counter sipping coffee. I was completely cool. I was in no way averting my eyes from the sight of his damp skin. I was definitely not going to allow myself to check how accurate my dream memory had been of his body. I was *fine.*

"You're up," he observed.

"Mmm-hmm." My voice was higher than usual, but not a squeak. "Coffee?"

"Please." He ran a hand through his hair. "Do I need a haircut?"

Why are you making me look at you? I thought. But that was not the reaction of someone who was fine, so I took a glance at his head. His light brown hair was definitely getting on the shaggy side, which was unusual for him. "I guess it's getting a little long."

"Mmm," was all he said. He padded barefoot to the kitchen to accept the cup of coffee I'd poured him.

"Go put some damn clothes on," I said, flicking my hand at him.

He grinned. "Why? Is all this—" he did a presenting gesture from shoulder to hip—"more than you can handle? Am I turning you on too much?"

I gave him a dirty look. "You're making me cold. It's cold in here." I crossed my arms over my chest for emphasis.

Beckett shrugged. "My body temperature has no bearing on yours." He took a deliberate sip of coffee, watching me with a spark of amusement in his eyes.

I refused to respond. I was certainly not going to admit that the very body he was presenting to me had raised my temperature pretty thoroughly just a short time ago. No way. I wouldn't give him the satisfaction. Or the ammunition against me for the future. And why should I say anything anyway? Because I was over it. O-V-E-R it. Nothing to see here folks, move it along. Emmy Black can have sex dreams about whomever the hell she wants, thank you very much. It's nobody's business but hers.

Which was a great internal pep talk and all, and it might have even worked if that was the only dream I ever had about him.

But it turned out to be just the first.

Damn. Damn. Damn.

BATHROOM BIRTHDAY PARTY FOR TWO

*I*t was the final day of Gross Anatomy. We'd been working on the intricacies of the head for the last week and a half, and today was the inner ear. The very last piece of the human puzzle. Mandy, Jon, and I all had stiff necks from bending over our cadaver. I was starting to think my neck and shoulders would never feel normal again after this semester. There was just so much bending! Hovering over the intricate nerves and vessels of the hands, dissecting out each muscle of the feet. I was bleary-eyed and exhausted by the end of each lab day.

But we only had one more presentation to get through, and Jon had the lead for it, so that was good. When we'd decided on the workload at the beginning of lab, I'd shamelessly pulled the Birthday Card. My birthday happened to fall on our last lab day, and I was not going to let that opportunity go to waste. I pleaded with Mandy and Jon to get one of them to take the final presentation, and Jon caved. Victory for Emmy!

"So we're going out celebrating tonight, right?" Jon asked, taking a momentary pause to stretch his neck.

"Hell yes," Mandy said. "I am so ready for this semester to be over."

"Best birthday present ever," I concurred.

"Speaking of that, what do you think Beckett's going to get you?" Mandy said.

Jon began to wiggle his butt and chant, "Birthday sex, birthday sex." Mandy laughed and began to dance with him.

That was one thing I was sure I wasn't getting for my 23rd birthday. "Ha ha," I said. "I don't know. We don't really make a big deal out of birthdays." It seemed like a good enough answer, considering I had zero expectations of my so-called husband. Last year, he'd gotten me a cement mixer shot at a bar for my birthday, which frankly I would have rather gone without.

"Let's meet at your place at, what? Nine?" Jon said. "We'll have a couple rounds before we go out."

"Because you're cheap?" Mandy teased.

"You call it cheap, I call it good economics."

"Yeah, yeah."

"Nine sounds fine," I said, to distract them.

And that was the end of our chatting, because our professor arrived at our table for our final presentation.

THAT EVENING, Beckett and I were in high spirits. We stopped in our favorite little taqueria on the way home from lab and ate our fill of their amazing tacos standing at one of the high counters in the shop's window, then we headed back to our apartment as a light snow began to fall from the sky.

There still wasn't any accumulation on the ground yet, which surprised me based on my image of the Midwest from movies. But so far we'd only had a few days of light snow that melted on contact. Today was huge, fluffy flakes that made the little town of River Glen look like a souvenir snow globe. It was gorgeous, despite the cold. I tried to catch flakes on my tongue, and managed to get one in my eye instead, which had us giggling for the last block before home.

Back in our little abode, I decided to grab a shower. Get the smell of the anatomy lab out of my hair for the last time. It was back to my turn in the bedroom, so I could actually strip out of my clothes in peace and head for the bathroom with my towel wrapped around me. Beckett was in the kitchen when I passed through, scrolling through something on his phone. Just as I closed the door behind me, I heard the electronic chirp of his phone connecting to the speaker. Music began to play as I turned on the shower. The noise of the water made it impossible to tell what song was on, but the backbeat was enough to have me grooving as I hung up my towel and got into the spray.

I was shaving my legs—pointless, maybe, but it was my birthday and I wanted to feel pretty—when the door suddenly burst open, so hard it slammed against the wall and rebounded, slamming just as hard into its jamb. I screamed.

"Sorry—fuck—I cut myself—" Beckett's voice was tense, even muffled by the sound of my shower. He had never, not even once, come into the bathroom while I was showering. I peeped my head around the curtain nervously and was greeted by the sight of blood.

Beckett stood at the sink, blood seeping out between his fingers as he squeezed his left thumb in his fist. Crimson streaks ran down his wrist and a thin trail of droplets dotted the floor. Absurdly, there was a bottle of champagne on the back of the toilet.

"Oh my god, what happened?"

"I was trying to get this ready to pop as soon as you came out and the fucking bottle opener...fuck." He winced, leaning his elbows on the edge of the sink.

"I'll help, just hold on." I turned off the water and snatched my towel from the hook, wrapping it around myself and tucking in

141

the end as tightly as I could. I stepped out of the tub and went to Beckett, putting my hands on his back. "I'm here. Let me look."

"It's not that bad." He sounded annoyed, but I didn't think it was with me.

"Let me see."

He eased his fingers open and revealed an impressive slice in the pad of his left thumb.

I sucked air through my teeth. "Jeez, how did you do that?"

"It was the fucking bottle opener—" he cut himself off with a grunt.

"Why were you using a bottle opener on champagne?" The question was out of my mouth before I could think better of it. Probably not the best time to second-guess someone.

He gave me a sour look. "I was using the knife part to get the foil off."

I let it go in favor of raiding the medicine cabinet for anything helpful. We didn't have much in the way of first aid, other than standard bandages and an old tube of antibiotic ointment. I figured paper towel and ice was better than anything we had in here and turned to go for the kitchen.

Which is when the bathroom doorknob pulled off in my hand.

And I watched in fascination as the long, thin bolt that connected the one in my hand to the one on the other side disappeared from the small hole. Outside the door, the matching knob hit the door with a clunk.

"Well...crap." I said.

"What?" Beckett asked.

"Um..." I turned, holding up the knob in explanation.

"Are you kidding me?"

"Nope."

He shook his head slowly. "We're stuck in here?"

I was struck with inspiration. "Which pocket is your phone in? I'll see if Ginny or Tom is home."

"My phone's connected to the speaker."

Duh. The music was still playing. "Mine's in the bedroom."

He laughed. Just once and without humor. "Of course it is."

"Never mind that for now. Let's get your hand taken care of."

Another run through the medicine cabinet and a search of the rest of the bathroom didn't yield much. But I got his thumb wrapped tightly in Kleenex and helped him clean the blood off his hands and wrists before I made him sit on the closed lid of the toilet with his hand above his head while I figured out the next move.

We were trapped inside with no phones, no window, and the music playing too loud for anyone to hear us shouting for help. But on the plus side, I knew for a fact that our friends were coming over at nine o'clock. So, we weren't going to die of starvation and be discovered when the neighbors started complaining about the smell. We weren't even going to be in here for long. But Beckett was injured, and I was...well, basically naked.

"So, I have to ask," I said when we had him situated. "Why did you bring the champagne in with you?"

He chuckled. "I didn't even know it was still in my hand. I just ran in here."

"Well, I think it's pretty obvious this is a sign, don't you?"

He twisted to retrieve the bottle from the top of the toilet tank and held it out to me. "I think it's safer for all of us if you do the honors."

I pursed my lips, regarding the bottle and the bloody hand print that was still on the label. "Mmm, biohazard vineyards, my favorite."

He grinned. "Oh, look who's squeamish all of a sudden."

It was hard to look intimidating in a towel, but I tried. "We have already established that there are many things I will do for you, Beckett. But I draw the line at vampirism."

"Fine." He sighed. "Rinse it off."

The bottle came clean easily in the sink. But that still left me with one obstacle. "There's, like, a 50-50 chance of my towel falling off if I have to work too hard at this cork."

He tried not to let me see, but there was definitely a hint of a smile on his face. "You can have my hoodie."

I helped him ease his bandaged hand through the sleeves and gratefully slipped on his big sweatshirt, zipping it up all the way to the top. I was still Porky Pigging it, but at least I wasn't clinging to a damp towel anymore. And the sweatshirt was long enough to cover me to the top of my thighs. Better than nothing.

And good enough for me to perch on the edge of the tub and clamp the champagne bottle between my knees. I squinched my face up, leaning away from the cork as I always did. Opening champagne freaked me out. But the top popped out with only a little fuss, and barely any gushed onto the floor.

"Happy birthday, Em." Beckett's tone said this was not exactly the champagne moment he'd had in mind.

But I tilted the bottle in his direction as a lame toast, said, "Cheers," and hoisted it to my lips. Then I offered it to him.

He took it with his uninjured hand and peered down the opening. "So, blood is a no, but saliva is a yes?"

"You have put your tongue in my mouth," I reminded him.

To my surprise and delight, red splotches rose on his cheekbones. He made a head tilt of acknowledgement and took a drink from the bottle.

"So now what?" he asked when he was done.

"Now we wait for someone to show up, and we kill this bottle of champagne."

"I'm in."

We had approximately three hours to burn before there was even the likelihood of rescue, and we quickly figured out there wasn't a whole lot to do in the bathroom. The first half hour or so was easy enough to pass. I had to get Beckett's thumb properly bandaged once the worst of the bleeding stopped. I also decided to go ahead and dry my hair and put on some makeup. We might be temporarily trapped, but that didn't mean we weren't going out after we were rescued.

With nothing else to do, Beckett watched me. I was hyperconscious of my naked ladybits every time I raised my arms, but I succeeded in not flashing him.

"How do girls learn how to do that?" he asked as I carefully sketched eyeliner along my upper lids.

"I learned from watching my mom. And YouTube."

"Huh." He stretched his mouth open in imitation when I put on my mascara. "Does that actually help?"

I laughed. "Shut up."

When I was finished, I turned to him with eyebrows lifted, as if he were the one to approve my work.

"Looks good," he said with a shrug.

"Gee thanks."

"What?"

"All that effort and all I get is a shrug?"

"I said you look good." He rolled his eyes. "You're beautiful, Em. You know that."

My heart swooped into my throat. I wasn't one of those girls people write pop songs about. You know, the ones who have no idea they're gorgeous? I wasn't super model material, but I knew I was okay to look at. But I didn't think Beckett had ever had an opinion about me. So I stammered something like "Oh, uh…I…oh."

Thank god for the bottle of champagne. I took a healthy swig just for something to do. And then I shamelessly changed the subject. "Who do you think is going to be the one to find us?"

We talked about that, and school, and our classmates, and California, and everything. There was nothing else to do. Eventually Beckett declared that he had to pee, so I stood in the shower with my hands over my ears and my eyes squeezed shut. It was totally childish; we had just spent an entire semester dissecting human bodies. I'd held a stranger's bladder in my hands. But somehow we both knew this was a line we were not going to cross. I made him do the same a little while later.

"At least we're not trapped in the bedroom," I said after I told him I was finished. "I probably would have wet my pants."

He laughed. "You're not wearing any pants."

The whole thing had given us a case of extremely immature giggles. Or maybe that was the champagne.

The edge of the tub was really starting to make my butt hurt, so I settled myself onto the floor in front of it. Not too long after, Beckett joined me. It was better having him next to me because I knew he couldn't see up the sweatshirt to my bare butt. We were both cold on the hard tile—he was down to a t-shirt after giving me his hoodie—and I found myself leaning into his shoulder for a little extra warmth. It was the first time I'd let myself be this close to him since he'd started starring in my sex dreams and it was…nice. Good to be near him again. He was the only person in my life who knew our secret, and I needed that.

We passed the bottle of champagne back and forth until it was empty. My head was fizzing with the oddly buoyant kind of drunk that only came from champagne.

"You know if you had told me back in Bio Sci 93 that I would spend my 23rd birthday locked in a bathroom, drinking champagne with my lab partner, I don't think I would have believed you."

"Is it the part about being locked in the bathroom, or your lab partner that you'd find hard to believe?"

"Yes."

"What about the part where you married your lab partner?" He extended his left hand, displaying his ring.

"That, too." I brought my left hand closer until our rings were aligned. Beckett stretched his fingers out, weaving between mine, then pulling them down for a brief squeeze. Like a hug.

"You wanna hear something I never told you?" he asked,

releasing my fingers.

"Yes."

"I thought you were so cute when you sat next to me in lab."

"You did?" It wasn't a huge confession, really, but it made my stomach feel warm and tingly.

"Yeah." He made it sound obvious. "I mean, shit, Em, you look at anybody with those big green eyes of yours and they're a goner."

I rolled my big green eyes. It was always the thing guys said first. "Uh-huh."

"That long hair, that face, that body...come on." He shrugged. "When I left Arizona, I wasn't sure I wanted to stay with Emily."

Now *that* was news. "Seriously?"

"Yeah. And then I saw you and I was like 'This is a sign.'" He rubbed the back of his head with his good hand. "And I was honestly trying to figure out the best way to hit on you when we introduced ourselves."

My heart fluttered and whirled in my chest. This was big time news. I couldn't speak.

Beckett laughed softly. "Aaaand then you said your name was Emily and I was like 'Oh fuck. This *is* a sign.'"

"Oh my god," I finally managed to say. "That's why you stayed with her?"

"That." He nodded, not looking at me. "And I'm lazy, I guess. Or maybe that's not the right word. I was comfortable. It was easy."

The more I learned about Emily, the less easy their relationship seemed to me. But maybe it had been easy, as long as she was six hours away. "Wow."

"Yeah, so there you go. I didn't hit on your because of your name, then I married you for the same reason four years later." He covered his eyes with one hand. "Pretty fucked up."

"Beck—"

"You don't have to say anything," he interrupted. "I probably shouldn't have told you. I don't want you to feel weird."

"No, no, I don't." I put one hand gently on his wrist, leading his hand away from his eyes. "I'm just sorry my name is Emily."

He looked puzzled.

"You wouldn't have had to go through hell with Emily if you'd broken up with her freshman year." I wondered what I might have said if he had come up with some kind of line to use on me that first day in lab. I'd thought he was cute, but I was very into keeping my options open in college. Would I have let him take me out? Would I have wanted to go out again, or would I have wanted to see who else was out there? Would we have ended up friends, and later roommates the way it really happened? It seemed unlikely we'd be here right now, married, on the floor in our bathroom, an empty bottle of champagne at our feet, and me wearing nothing but his sweatshirt.

Beckett's blue eyes met mine. "I think maybe things happen the way they're supposed to," he said softly.

"So we were supposed to get stuck in the bathroom tonight?"

"Maybe."

The air around us suddenly seemed alive with electricity, and I felt as though I didn't dare blink.

"I think maybe we were supposed to be friends..." he swallowed, "first."

First? The word had such weight. Such consequence. Did he mean before we got married? Or something else? Champagne made it hard for me to think my way to the right question. I knew I should ask...something. Our situation was already so convoluted, there was no room for a word so open to interpretation as *first*. But what I wanted to do was see what he would do if I kissed him.

I flicked my gaze to his lips. What did he mean by *first*?

"Emmy?" A voice called from the other side of the door. "Beckett?"

My heart sank. Our rescuers had arrived.

21

AM I CRAZY?

*E*veryone thought our situation was hilarious. It had been Mandy who arrived first. Mandy who had responded to our shouts and pounding on the door. Mandy who fed the bolt through the hole in the door and held fast while I jiggled mine back into place. But you would have sworn that everyone had already been there by the end of the night. Everyone wanted their part in the story.

There were warnings to be careful every time one of us went off to a bathroom. Suggestions about not forgetting to wear pants. And endless teasing about how we must have been really going at it to knock the doorknob clean off. Not to mention much admiration for Beckett for bringing champagne into the bathroom.

I accepted more birthday shots than I should have, and by the time we hit a third bar, I had the spins. Beckett made me switch to water then, and didn't give in even when everyone booed him.

Somehow everyone else seemed to be in better shape than me —a lack of birthday shots, I suspect—and a bunch of people were playing darts in the back of the bar. Reina managed to snag a table and I gratefully dropped into a chair.

"Oh my god, I haven't been this fucked up since undergrad," I announced.

"You mean all of five months ago?" Travis teased. He was one of the older members of our class, having been a corpsman in the Navy before he went to school.

"Shush, it was a long time ago." I propped my head on my hands, wishing desperately that I wasn't so drunk for just a minute.

Beckett appeared at my shoulder with a fresh cup of ice water, which I took gratefully. "Thank you."

"Just drink it all. I'll be back with another."

"Aww," Reina cooed when he was gone. "He takes such good care of you."

I nodded. "He does."

"I was talking to my mom after Thanksgiving, and she told me I should find myself a man like him. She thinks he's one of the good ones."

I nodded again. "He is." My head bobbed a bit when I turned to look for Beckett, but I managed not to let it fall onto the table. There he was, standing near the wall while Jon took his turn at the dart board. He glanced my direction, and saw me looking. He pantomimed drinking and pointed to my water. I picked up the cup, draining the last of the liquid and sucking up an ice cube to boot. He smiled and winked.

Yeah, he was one of the good ones. I could see it. He was kind, caring, patient, fun, smart. And he was only going to be mine for a little longer. Not that he was really mine at all. But soon enough he'd be a free agent again. Theoretically, Reina could have not just a man *like* Beckett, she could have Beckett himself.

The thought made my throat ache.

Somewhere along the way, he'd really started to feel like mine. I couldn't say when, or how. Maybe it was all the acting. Like rehearsing a play. If you read the lines over and over, you started to identify with your character. Maybe I'd simply tricked myself into thinking Beckett felt like more than a friend. Method acting with disastrous results.

How would I ever be able to know for sure?

God, I was too intoxicated to find my way out of a paper bag. I could not be expected to muddle through my non-existent love life.

Beckett materialized at my shoulder again with a fresh glass of water. He didn't say anything, just set it in front of me, and started to walk away. Impulsively, I grabbed his hand. He looked down, concern on his face.

I shook my head. "Nothing."

He stroked my hair with his other hand, wounded thumb extended for safety. "When you're ready, I'll take you home."

I looked him in the eyes. "Take me home."

~

WE CALLED a ride service to get home. The snow, which had been so beautiful in the afternoon, was finally starting to stick. I was fascinated by the flakes swirling in the headlights of the car, leaning into the middle to look between the headrests at the display. Beside me, Beckett put his hand on the seat, palm up, and I decided not to second- and third-guess myself before I settled my hand in his. We were both wearing gloves, but it didn't matter.

The snow was driving down hard on the short walk from the car to the building, and we were both covered when we stepped into the foyer.

Beckett smiled at me. "There's snow in your eyelashes."

Stupidly, I tried to look at my own lashes, but failed.

"They're already gone," he said softly and peeled off his gloves to wipe the melting flakes from my cheekbones.

I shivered and grabbed his wrists. "Beckett..." But I didn't know what else to say, and after a moment's hesitation, he dropped his hands from my face and led the way up to our apartment. There was no trouble with the keys this time, and soon we were inside.

For a few minutes, I let him go about his business, putting his coat away while I wiggled out of mine. He didn't speak or look me in the eye as he took my coat from me to hang it up. Then he stopped in the bedroom to grab his pajamas before disappearing into the bathroom, pausing only long enough to rattle the doorknob a few times to ensure it was still connected. I didn't know what else to do but follow the same path.

In the bedroom, I let the door close but not latch while I struggled drunkenly out of my clothes. I felt restless and let down as I tried to figure out which end was up on my pajama shirt. This was the night I'd tried to wingman him all over again. This was Mandy arriving just when the air was starting to crackle earlier tonight.

This was what *should* be happening, I tried to remind myself. We were roommates. We were friends. We had baggage and a big fat secret between us. Being drunk was not a good time to be making any kind of decisions about anything, much less about a situation as delicate as ours.

But it wasn't what I wanted to be happening.

The bathroom clicked open, and I scurried to the door, forgetting I wasn't wearing pants. Again. I had once chance, I told myself.

They didn't call it liquid courage for nothing, right?

"Beckett," I said, and he went still, his back to me.

"What?"

"Can I ask you something?"

"Depends on what you want to ask, I guess." He turned enough to show me his profile.

I walked slowly toward him, pulling him by the arm until he turned.

There were so many questions I wanted to ask: How will I

ever know if you stop faking what you feel for me? Do you still miss Emily? Did you feel it earlier? The spark? Was I the only one who felt it? What did you mean that we were meant to be friends *first*? Do you really not miss sex?

But I didn't ask any of that. I blurted out, "Am I crazy?"

"What? Why?"

"I thought before, in the foyer, and before that in the bathroom, and maybe at the bar, the second bar, not the third, did we go to a third? No, yeah, the third. And then in the car, but also before that, maybe even at Reina's house. I thought...I thought maybe there was something—that you wanted to, or maybe you were just thinking maybe you wanted to—to—but now...am I crazy?"

Beckett closed his eyes for a moment, then looked at me. The word that came to my befuddled mind was *intent.* He brought his hand up to cup my cheek, and he leaned in, so close I had to shut my eyes or the nearness of him would have made me dizzy. And I felt the barest skim of his stubbled cheek against me, and then he nuzzled his nose on mine.

"You're not crazy, Emmy."

A sound I have never made before came out of me. It was something like a sigh, but also a quavering cry. It was relief, and longing, and nervousness all at once. I had to grab onto him, my hand curling around his biceps, just to stop myself from falling, or flying off into space.

Beckett sighed. "But tonight, I'm going to put you to bed, okay?"

"No," I protested weakly.

"You've had a lot to drink," he said softly, rubbing his thumb up and down my cheek. "And I'm not going to be that guy."

"Unh," I whimpered. "Why do you have to be so good? I don't want to be good."

"Trust me," he said. "I don't want to fuck this up, okay?"

"Beckett, please..." I stepped closer, invading his space, laying my hands on his chest. His heart thumped against my palm. The spark was everywhere, lighting me up all the way down to my chilly toes. I tilted my head up, finding the underside of his chin with first my nose, then my lips. I didn't kiss him, not for real, just grazed my lips along his jaw.

He grabbed my hips, his fingers digging into my flesh. "Emmy...fuck."

I slid my hands up his shoulders to the back of his neck and tipped his head down until I could reach his lips if I stood on my toes. When he spoke again, we were so close that his lips brushed against mine with each syllable.

"I have a lot of will power. A lot. But you have to go to bed, Emmy. You are killing me."

I groaned, but released him. "Okay. Okay. For you."

"Thank you."

22

THE MORNING AFTER

*M*y head wasn't aching nearly as much as it probably deserved to when I opened my eyes in the morning. And my stomach only had a slightly sour feeling instead of the nausea I would have expected. Beckett and his magic water cure.

Beckett.

Oh god.

He'd sent me to bed last night like an overtired toddler on a sugar high. Oh god. What must he think of me? How badly had I embarrassed myself? I tried to remember what I'd said to him, but I couldn't untangle the words that had come out of my mouth from those that had been trapped in my head. And what had he said to me?

You're not crazy, Emmy.

Well great. Not super helpful. Were those words that he said to calm down the babbling drunk girl? Between that and the mystery of *first* while we were in the bathroom, I didn't know what was going on in his head.

I shook my head with a moan. This is why shots were always a bad idea. I did not make good decisions while drinking shots.

The clock read 7:18. Great. I hadn't even managed to sleep in. Beckett and his magic water cure wreaked havoc on the bladder. And now my tangled thoughts were going to keep me from falling back to sleep. Worst of all, Beckett was on the other side of the door. Because why not have to confront your idiocy first thing in the morning?

Please let him be asleep, I thought as I tiptoed out of bed. He was, thank god.

I ninja'd my way to the bathroom and nearly cheered when the doorknob stayed in place. I peed, then stared at my reflection while I washed my hands. My hair was a fright show, and my eyeliner had spread out like it was trying to start a colony under my eyes. I made a yuck face at myself and caught a glimpse of green in my mouth. The crayon-bright color of my tongue reminded me that I'd been drinking something called Dirty Girl Scouts last night. Creme de menthe and Irish cream. Tasty, but wow, this was a gross side effect. I decided to brush my teeth.

Then there was nothing left for me to do but go back into the living room. I crossed my fingers and sent up a prayer that Beckett would still be zonked out on the futon.

Nope.

He was sitting on the edge, elbows propped on his knees, staring straight at me when I came out.

"Hi," I said, freezing like a deer in the headlights.

"Hungover?" he asked.

I shook my head. "Not bad. Thanks for all the water."

"What do you remember from last night?"

Oh god. The acid in my stomach turned into a tidal wave. I swallowed hard. "All of it."

"You sure?"

Now my heart was paddling desperately on the tidal wave, trying not to drown. I nodded. "I'm sure."

"Good." He stood and crossed the room in three strides before he captured my face in his hands and kissed me. And it wasn't the dry, chaste kiss from our wedding, or the over-the-top kisses for show at the barbecue from the day we moved in; it was a breath-stealing, toe-curling, stomach-dropping kiss. It was a kiss that refused to give up its hold. That begged me to quit oxygen for just a few minutes, please. I could live without breathing, surely, if he would just keep kissing me forever.

Beckett's hands slid over my shoulders and down my back, grabbing my butt and lifting me until I wrapped my legs around his waist. I wanted to cry with relief, and laugh, but more than that I never wanted to stop kissing him. He carried me to the bedroom, and lay me back on the sheets, kissing me all the while.

When his body settled onto mine, I finally broke the kiss with a gasp. The weight and heat of him was so much better in real life than in any dream. He fit against me in all the right places, and left me aching for him to fill in any gaps.

"Are you all right?" he asked.

"God yes." I rolled my hips against him.

"That was the longest night of my life," he said.

"I thought—"

He cut me off with another kiss.

"I told you you weren't crazy."

Hungrily, I pulled him in, winding my arms around his chest, as if I could draw him beneath my skin if I just tried hard enough. I was embarrassingly desperate. Not just because of the long dry spell, or the dreams that left me unsatisfied. But because it was Beckett here with me, and Beckett whose mouth was exploring the soft spot below my ear. My friend. My husband who I was definitely supposed to be sharing an apartment with, not DNA.

I managed to form a question: "Are you sure you want to do this?"

"I would have thought that was obvious."

"No, I mean…" I couldn't think clearly. My body was made of lava and electricity. "I mean us. I don't want to make things weird."

He laughed and rubbed the tip of my nose with his. "Yeah, wouldn't want to make our very normal marriage weird."

"What if—what if—?"

"Do you want to stop?" He went still, lifting his weight off me slightly.

I arched my back, seeking contact between us again. "No. I just—I'm nervous." I couldn't believe I'd said it. He was either going to hit the brakes, or tease me.

Instead he said, "Me, too," in a soft voice. "It's okay. It's just me."

"That's what makes me nervous."

"Think of it this way, I've only been with a girl who said we were going to hell the first time I got her in bed. I will be very easy to impress."

A little spark of anger lit in my belly. Not at him. At Emily. He deserved so much better than what she'd given him. He was one of the good ones, damn it. He'd taken care of me, and made sure I wouldn't regret what I did last night. He put me to bed when I fell asleep on the couch. He duct taped up a shower curtain for me when I felt too grubby to sleep. He bought me tacos on my birthday, and he held me when I cried. He deserved the best.

I looked into his eyes. "Oh, I'm not just going to impress you. I'm going to rock your fucking world."

Maybe it wasn't the most romantic thing I could have said, but it was a mission statement, and I intended to deliver. I pushed him down to the bed, swinging my leg over to straddle him. There was a fire in his eyes and I'm sure it was mirrored in mine.

This was happening. For weeks, I'd been questioning my own feelings. Wondering if it was all in my head. And now, here was the reality. I wanted Beckett. Bad. I wanted to rock his world.

"What do you like?" I asked, because I would give it to him in spades.

"I—don't know?" His answer and his uncertainty were almost sweet.

"Well, let's find out then." I smiled, and tugged his t-shirt up to slide my hands beneath and explore all the beautiful territory I'd been unable to touch all this time. Beckett's eyes went heavy and he stretched under my hands like a happy cat. "You like."

"I like."

"Okay then." We carried on like that, with me checking his reaction to everything. Turned out, there wasn't much he didn't like. My hands anywhere on his body? He liked. My lips marking a path down his stomach? He liked. My tongue? He really liked. And he liked touching and kissing and licking my body as he stripped off my stupid UC-I Anteaters shirt and the cotton panties with SMARTY PANTS written across the butt, which was probably the least sexy thing I could possibly have worn for this moment.

But Beckett didn't care. He knelt beside my naked body and ran a hand from the notch between my collar bones to my pubic bone, making me squirm at the delicate touch. Every inch of me tingled with want. "Are you still okay with this?" he asked.

"God, yes."

I sent up a prayer of thanks to the gods of sex that I had kept a condom in my underwear drawer that hadn't expired. Beckett looked startled when I started to roll it on him.

"You're very full service," he said.

"This way I know it's done right." And with that same attitude, I pushed him back on the bed and once again straddled his hips. "Are you ready for me?"

"Oh, fuck yes."

We slid together, and the intense feeling of fullness had me seeing stars for a second. Holy crap, it had been a long time since I'd done this. I closed my eyes, letting my head drop back as I waited for the initial tightness to ease.

"Are you okay?" he asked.

"Yyyyeeeessss. I'm very, very okay."

"Thank god."

I opened my eyes, giving him a quizzical look.

"I might have actually cried if you'd said we had to stop."

I laughed, and he grinned. The vibrations of my laughter went all through me, down to the place where we were joined. It made me jump, which only made me laugh again, and this time Beckett started laughing too.

We were still giggling when I started to move, and even after the giggles subsided, we smiled at each other like idiots. But then I found an angle that made my eyelids flutter and we weren't such dorks anymore. Now I was watching his face, and the way his lips fell open and a little pair of lines that appeared between his eyebrows as the pleasure built.

His hands found my hips, gripping tight. I dropped to my elbows so I could kiss him again, craving even more connection between us.

No surprise, we were both on pretty short fuses. Soon, Beckett's pace told me he was running out of time. I sat up so I could put one hand between us, touching myself to make sure he wasn't the only one on the home stretch.

He looked down in surprise, then up at me. "Oh fuck, that's hot."

We were both breathing fast and hard, and then he stopped breathing altogether for a few seconds and I knew he was about to finish. I increased the tempo of my fingers, but he beat me to it. I didn't care. It was amazing to watch him. And being a very quick and receptive student, he held perfectly still inside me while I took myself over the edge just a couple moments after.

The orgasm bowled through me, and I collapsed onto his chest. He held me, kissing my face.

"You all right?" he asked.

"Mmm-hmm."

"Let me see you."

I pushed myself up to my elbows, finding his eyes filled with concern. I smiled, knowing it had to be a goofy smile. "Stop worrying, you silly boy."

"Sorry." He sighed, then chuckled. "That was...wow. I didn't know it could be like that."

"You know what this means, right?" I said.

"What?"

"Now we have to get married." It was a dangerous joke to make, but if I knew Beckett...

He burst out laughing.

23

LOST AND FOUND

*W*e got lost that weekend. Took no notice of anything or anyone but each other. It was like we'd broken a dam. There was so much to make up for. All the times I'd felt the touch of his hand on my lower back, or gotten a swift kiss on the head? Those could have been his hands sliding around my waist and his lips on my neck. There could have been nights of falling asleep in each other's arms.

It wasn't just the physical, either. As much as I'd thought I knew Beckett, there was so much more. We talked endlessly. Nothing was off limits.

"Does it make me a bad person if I wish my parents would just get a divorce?" We were lying in bed in the middle of Sunday afternoon, having just had what was probably some very weird sex during which we tried to name every nerve that was involved in the process. Turns out, it's very hard to remember things *in flagrante delicto*. And that we were way weirder than I'd thought.

"Not if they're not happy together."

He sighed, tucking a piece of my hair behind my ear. "They're not. But then I wonder if they're just unhappy people. What if they're, like, happy being miserable together?"

"I hope not. That sounds awful."

"Yeah."

I bit my lip, and decided to go ahead with something that had been on my mind for a while now. "Can I ask? Why did you want to get married when your parents are so unhappy? Didn't you worry?"

"Well, yeah," he said as if it were obvious. "But, you know, you sort of think you'll do it differently than they did. Get it right."

"Even though you didn't really want to do it?"

"I know. It sounds crazy. But it didn't seem like a big deal. Like, do it now or do it later, what's the difference?"

"Very romantic, Beck."

"Says the girl who married me to avoid being homeless."

"That was a business arrangement."

He shrugged. "So was marrying Emily. I don't know, I guess I figured worst case scenario, we'd be no worse off than my parents."

"Aspiring to be the same level as miserable as your parents is not a life goal."

"I wasn't. I was just preparing for the worst while hoping for the best."

"Still fucked up."

"Yeah, well…" He left the words hanging.

"Of course, what do I know? Maybe you're right. My parents were very happy together, and look what happened."

"Em, no."

"I'm just saying. Maybe it's just as crazy to want to be happy."

Beckett rolled up to one elbow, looking down at me. "It's not crazy."

"But you can lose it all in a heartbeat."

"At least you had it once, though, right? At least you know it's possible."

"I guess."

"It is. Trust me." He leaned in to kiss me. "The six of us, living

163

in our house in Irvine? That was the first time I knew it was possible to just be happy."

I reached up to smooth my palm over his cheek, the feeling of pity in my chest too strong not to touch him.

"So that's what I want now. I don't want to be unhappy. It's not easier. It's worse. Way worse."

My entire chest felt like it was throbbing. I wanted to hurt everyone who had ever hurt Beckett. He didn't deserve that. He was one of the good ones. I didn't know how, given his background, but he'd done better than his parents. He was good.

I pulled him close, until his forehead rested against mine. "I want you to be happy."

He smiled. "Then shut up and kiss me."

~

LATER WE HAD TO PACK. There was a flight to catch in the morning. We were both Phoenix-bound, though for different reasons. Beckett was going home to meet his fate with his family, whatever that would be. I was meeting my dad there because it had been a cheap ticket for both of us. When you don't have a home, it doesn't really matter where you spend the holiday. It had been a toss-up between Phoenix and Salt Lake City, and at least this way I'd have someone to sit with on the plane.

"You should bring your dad to my house," Beckett said.

"Yeah, you've done a great job of selling a family Christmas with the Andersons," I teased. "Where do I sign up?"

"I just feel bad that you'll be spending Christmas in a hotel."

I shrugged. "It's practically a family tradition." This would be the fourth Christmas my dad and I had spent at a restaurant or a hotel, though the first outside of California.

"Well, you're invited, okay?" He held up a hand. "Only if you want to."

"Hey, everybody, remember my friend Emmy from undergrad? We're secretly married! Isn't that fun?"

"I *might* leave that part out," he admitted.

"Why?"

He threw a balled-up t-shirt at me.

"You're gonna have to figure out how to get that ring off your finger, then."

"Right."

We consulted Ye Olde Google and found a video about winding dental floss around your finger to get a tight ring off. It actually worked really well. Mine slid off easily, and we put both in the velvet box mine came in, which I tucked into my underwear drawer. In the exact spot where the lone condom had been.

My hand felt naked without my ring and I found my thumb searching for it repeatedly. "So weird," I said.

"Definitely."

Neither of us said anything else about it, but I caught Beckett rubbing his bare ring finger as often as I was while we finished our packing and got ready for bed. The transition from studiously avoiding impropriety with him to standing at the sink brushing our teeth together in our underwear was surprisingly smooth. Like turning a puzzle piece that didn't seem to fit before and finding it belonged there all along.

We went to bed later than we should have, considering the long drive to Des Moines before our early flight, but that still didn't stop us from finding each other in the dark, beneath the blankets. After the long dry spell, this weekend had taken a toll. Neither of us were up for another round, but that didn't mean there weren't plenty of other things to do.

"I'm going to miss you," Beckett said, palming my breast.

"Are you talking to me or my boob?"

"You." He laughed. "Mostly."

"It's only going to be two days." But I understood. I'd miss him too. I would have missed him even if we hadn't started sleeping together. I told him that.

"Me, too."

That was the last thing I remembered before I fell asleep.

24

FAMILY REUN-YUCK

*T*hree-thirty in the morning is a cruel time to wake up, but we had to get on the road to catch our flight. Neither of us spoke much on the drive to Des Moines, except when I checked to see if he was staying awake okay. The gas station coffee he was drinking smelled burned even to me. I didn't know how he was getting it down. But we made it, safe and sound, to a sparsely populated airport. It was Christmas Eve, pre-dawn, and the sensible people had done their traveling over the weekend.

We were the cheap people.

Still it meant we weren't fighting the crowds through security, and there were plenty of seats at the gate. Even the plane wasn't completely full, and we got a row of three to ourselves. With the arm rests up, I snuggled under Beckett's arm and the two of us fell asleep.

In Phoenix, I found a text message waiting for me from my dad. He'd arrived and was waiting for me in the baggage area. I was glad he'd flown in rather than brought his Harley. I knew how to ride on the back of it, but I hated it. I always felt like I was on the verge of death. Plus the helmet smelled weird.

"My dad will be at the baggage area," I said as Beckett and I walked past the security line. "So say goodbye to me here."

He pulled me aside and kissed me so thoroughly, I actually went weak in the knees.

I smiled at him when he let me go. "Hey, if your family is making you crazy, you know where to find me."

"I do."

We walked hand-in-hand to the escalators that would take us down to baggage, but then I knew it was time to let go. It wasn't that my dad was one of those get-your-hands-off-my-daughter types. But there was an awful lot I didn't want to explain to him just now. And as I could have predicted, he was waiting right at the bottom for me.

"There's my baby girl!" he called as soon as he spotted me.

"Hi dad!" I ran to him and jumped into his open arms. He lifted me right off my feet and squeezed me so hard I saw spots. When I was back on the ground, he held me at arm's length. "Look at you. God, it's good to see you."

"It's good to see you, too." Unexpectedly, my eyes stung. This was the longest I'd gone without seeing him, and it was giving me all the feels. *Not now*, I told myself. *Don't get all blubbery now.* I turned to re-introduce my dad to Beckett, but what I saw stopped me cold.

Beckett was looking off to the left, motionless, while other passengers made annoyed detours around him. It wasn't hard to see why he'd frozen in place, though. About twenty yards away stood a woman I recognized from graduation weekend as Beckett's mom, and beside her was a younger woman whose face I would have known from dozens of photographs even if I hadn't met her a few times over the years. Honey-colored hair, brown eyes, pretty face.

Emily fucking Wilson.

His mom smiled and crossed the space between them to hug his stiff body. "Welcome home, honey."

I couldn't hear what he said, but his expression told me it was something like "What is she doing here?"

I grabbed my dad by the arm and dragged him over to the action. "Dad, you remember my friend Beckett? And this is his mom, Mrs. Anderson."

"Nice to see you both," my dad said, offering his hand out for a shake.

Beckett's transfixed gaze loosened and he gave my dad a handshake.

"Hi, Mr. Black. Mom, you remember Emmy."

"Emmy, yes. One of the roommates," Mrs. Anderson said, leaning in to give me a kiss on the cheek. I wanted to push her away and wipe my cheek. "You're the one who's also at Middlesex."

"That's me." I gritted my teeth.

"It's so nice that you both had a friend at your new school." She smiled. It seemed like a genuine smile. She was probably being nice. But all I could see was a woman who had blindsided her son at the airport with the girl who'd called off their wedding.

Speaking of whom, Emily had slowly approached us and now stood slightly behind Mrs. Anderson. "Hey, Beckett," she said softly.

"What are you doing here?" His tone was deadly.

"I wanted to see you," she said.

"Now, Beckett, just give her a chance—" Mrs. Anderson put her hand on his arm.

"No," he said.

"Please," Emily said. "I just want to talk."

"No," he said again.

I wanted to tell her to get out. Go away. Leave him alone, for the love of god. She'd done enough. I looked at my dad with undisguised panic. His eyes were darting between the rest of us as he tried to assess the situation.

"I've invited the Wilsons over for our Christmas Eve gathering," Mrs. Anderson said with a smile that didn't meet her eyes.

"You did what?" Beckett demanded.

"They've been coming for years, honey, of course I did."

"You have got to be kidding me." Beckett rubbed his eyes with a steepled hand. I wanted to put my arms around him, soothe him with promises that he didn't have to go. That I would make Emily Wilson and her family stay away. But I couldn't touch him. I wasn't even supposed to be part of this awful tableau.

"I've missed you, Beckett," Emily added in a small voice.

Fuck you, I thought, glaring at her. She didn't even notice.

"You've got a weird way of showing it," he muttered.

"Beck..." I couldn't help it. I had to say something.

He looked at me, his face a swirling storm of a million emotions.

I bit my lip, dying to offer some comfort, but we were now in an upside-down world where we had to pretend to be nothing to each other. These were the people on the other side of our secrets.

"I invited Emmy and her dad for tonight," Beckett said suddenly, turning his intense blue eyes on his mother. "They're in Phoenix for the holiday, and I said they should come over."

"Uhh," my dad started to speak but I squeezed his wrist. He got me and shut his mouth. I was going to owe him some explanation later, but for now I was grateful to him for playing along.

"Well, certainly," Mrs. Anderson gave us a brief smile. "The more the merrier. Especially at Christmas!"

"Well, thank you very much," my dad said. "It would be an honor to join you." He offered up his hand for a second time. "John Black."

"Melanie Anderson."

"And I'm sorry, I don't think I caught your name." My dad turned his attention to Emily, extending his hand to her.

"Emily Wilson," she said. "I'm Beckett's..."

"Fiancée," Mrs. Anderson said.

"No she's not," Beckett cut in sharply.

Emily flinched, but managed a wobbly smile. "We were going to get married, but uh…"

In a falsely jovial tone, Beckett finished her opener, "But she called it off and we haven't spoken since." He shrugged and forced a laugh. "Fun, huh?"

"Uhh…" my dad said again.

"Don't be rude," Mrs. Anderson chided her son.

"You're the one who brought her."

She regrouped with a quick inhale and tried a new tack. "Emily, Emmy—oh I never realized how similar—sorry, I believe you two have met?"

"Yes, hi," Emily said with a shy smile. "Nice to see you again. H-how's Iowa?"

"Cold," I said.

"Oh goodness is that the time?" Mrs. Anderson made a show of looking at the clock. "We really do have to get going. Guests coming! We'll see you all at the house, soon, all right?" She smiled at my dad and me. "Do you have the address?"

I had a renewed desire to hit her. She was acting like this was a play set in Edwardian England, and we would all just defer to the proper etiquette. Like she hadn't ambushed her son with the girl who left him.

But my dad jumped right into his role, saying, "If you're sure it's no trouble. Is there anything we can bring? Emmy, do you have the address?"

"Beckett can text it to me."

"That's settled then. How wonderful. No need to bring anything. You're our guests." Mrs. Anderson gave us one final smile, and put her hand on Beckett's shoulder to shepherd him out.

I looked at him. My friend, my temporary husband, and now my—what? my lover? God, what an awful word. But here we

171

were, brand new to this part of our relationship, and he was being pushed into a maelstrom. Pushed toward the girl he'd intended to marry just months ago.

My chin started to quiver as I watched him walk away. No, no, no. I could not cry. Not in this stupid airport, and not in front of my father. I already had enough explaining to do.

Beckett looked back over his shoulder at me and mouthed, "I'm sorry."

I forced a smile and whispered, "It's okay."

But it wasn't okay.

I was terrified.

25

FELIZ NAVIDADDY

"So..." my dad drawled when we were alone, "you wanna tell me what the hell that was about?"

"I don't suppose no is an option?"

He shook his head.

I looked in the direction where Beckett had disappeared, chewing my lower lip anxiously. "Well, you caught the basics. Beckett was engaged to Emily, but she broke it off. And now his mom is apparently trying to play matchmaker. Or re-matchmaker, I guess."

"U-huh." He put a hand my back, guiding me toward the rental car garage. "And how did we get involved in this little family drama?"

"Beckett invited us." That was true. He'd even invited me while we were still back in River Glen. "I swear, I had no idea that Emily was going to be here." That was also true. I was killing this honesty thing! "And he's my friend. How can I make him face this all alone?" So many truths.

My dad nodded as we walked through the sliding doors to the noisy pick-up area outside. Between the sound of planes, shuttle buses, and the nearby freeway, I could barely hear myself think, much less have a discussion with him. So we walked in silence until we got to the Hertz garage. He'd checked in before I arrived, so all we had to do was get in the car.

I tossed my backpack in the trunk and pulled out my phone to text Beckett, *Are you okay?* then anxiously sat in the front seat, picking at my cuticles, waiting for him to respond.

My dad programmed our hotel address into the GPS and followed the voice's directions to get on the highway. I stared at my phone, but no messages came through.

"Emmy."

"Mmm?"

"You think you can tear your eyes away from the screen long enough to talk to your dad?"

Guilt made me tuck the phone under my thigh, where I'd be sure to feel even the slightest vibration. "Sorry."

He asked me how my flight had been, if I'd had an okay Thanksgiving, and how my classes had gone. I tried really hard to stay present, even though half my brain was focused on my hidden phone. Why wasn't Beckett answering? What was going on? What was Emily saying to him? Was he listening?

"I can't believe you willingly left your Harley in Alaska," I said when we hit a lull in our conversation.

"It's an awfully long ride through Canada *and* the United States in December."

"Still. That bike is basically your home."

He made an indistinct, hesitant sound.

"What does that mean?"

He sighed, then kind of laughed. "Well…I was hoping to tell you this in a little better circumstance than the car, but, uh…well, things with Charlene are pretty serious."

I didn't want to be hurt, but I couldn't help feeling a twinge of pain. That gut reaction of *How can he do this to mom?* I looked out the window. "Oh?"

"She's really wonderful, baby girl. I know you'll like her."

174

"That's great." My tone wasn't as enthusiastic as I'd hope to fake.

"Emmy, I know what you must be thinking."

"I'm just tired."

"I still miss your mom every day. Nothing will ever change that."

I picked at another cuticle. "I miss her, too."

"I really let you down, Em. I know that now."

I looked over in surprise. "What are you talking about?"

"When your mom died, I was...I was crushed. You'd gone off to college just the year before and then she was gone. I'd never felt so alone. That's why I sold the house. I couldn't stand to be surrounded by all the memories of you two."

"I was just in Irvine."

"I know that. But I knew you needed to lead your life. You needed to focus on school. A twenty-year-old isn't supposed to prop up her dad." He sighed. "And I know I probably let you lead that life a little too much on your own. You had your friends, lots of people around you, and I let that feel like enough. I should have been there for you more."

My eyes burned like I'd gotten hand sanitizer in them, and my voice was thin and quiet. "No, dad. I'm the one who should have been there for you more."

He patted my knee. "It wasn't your job. That's a parent's job."

I couldn't say anything more. There were too many tears rolling down my face. When I didn't speak again, my dad looked over at me.

"Oh baby girl, I'm sorry."

We were in the middle of a busy road with no way to stop, so all he could do was pat my knee. The GPS began agitatedly warning us that a left turn was coming up in a half mile, then 600 feet, then 200 feet. I wanted to take a hammer to the thing before it stopped advising my dad not to miss the stupid turn. Luckily it was the last turn, and within a minute, we were in the parking lot of our hotel.

My dad found the first available space and threw the car in park, unbuckling his seat belt so he could slide closer and give me a hug. "Don't cry, sweetheart. You know I hate it when you cry."

Someday, men will learn that telling a girl not to cry is basically an instruction to do the opposite. Today was obviously not that day, though, as I hugged my dad and cried and he told me not to cry over and over again. He said it in the same tone he'd used when I was a little girl with a fever, or a bee sting. The same tone he'd used when my first boyfriend had broken up with me in my sophomore year of high school. It was the familiarity, not the words themselves that were the comfort.

When I finally had control of myself, I sat back a bit and wiped my eyes with the back of my wrist, sniffling. "I"m sorry. I didn't mean to go all crazy on you."

"You're not crazy," he said, unknowingly echoing Beckett.

I couldn't resist sneaking a look at my phone, but there was still no response.

"You're really worried about your friend," my dad observed.

"Yeah."

"He's a big boy. I'm sure he's doing fine." He finally killed the rental car's engine. "Now what do you say we go check in?"

"Okay."

The hotel was nothing remarkable. Clean, and recently updated. The kind of place that doesn't give you the willies and doesn't make your jaw drop. I guess that might seem cold and anonymous for Christmas time, but I didn't mind. There was a big tree in the lobby and Christmas music playing softly in the background. And I was with my dad, which was really all I expected out of the holiday.

We checked into our room and my dad let me go into the bathroom to do some repair work on my mascara after the crying jag in the car. When I emerged, he'd gotten a recommendation for a local Tex-Mex place from the front desk.

"You still want to keep up our tradition, even with this invite to the family drama party?" he asked.

My family wasn't traditional. I was an only child of an only child (my mom) and a youngest child (my dad) whose family lived on the other side of the country. My mother was a terrible cook, and my dad's culinary achievements were limited to the field of breakfast. They were both workaholics who'd been deep in Silicon Valley during the early dot com days, so my concept of the holidays had never included crackling fires, homemade gingerbread houses, or turkey with all the trimmings. What we did have was a Christmas Eve tradition of going out for Mexican food. It was pretty much the only constant from year to year, and the only thing my dad and I had maintained after my mother's death.

"Of course I do!" I said.

He smiled broadly.

~

THE MEXICAN PLACE was a little storefront in a strip mall, but the salsa was made in-house and the margaritas were delicious. Our conversation was easier now, and I told him more about the new friends I'd made in Iowa. He tried and failed not to cringe when I talked about Gross Anatomy and how I weirdly missed our cadaver now that he'd been sent off for cremation.

"We named him Gary," I said.

"I still don't understand how you can like this stuff," he admitted.

I shrugged. "I don't understand how you can look at computer code all day."

"Computer code never smells or spills on your pants."

I laughed.

We talked about Alaska and Canada. His eyes lit up talking about the area. He couldn't wait for me to come up to see him there.

"Will you actually be staying long enough for that to happen?" I asked.

"Like I said, things have gotten pretty serious with Charlene, so...yeah, I'd say I'm staying put for now."

"Wow." Tears pricked at the back of my eyes again, but it didn't hurt so bad now. "I guess I'll have to meet her, huh?"

"I'd really like that."

We talked about when I might be able to come to visit. It would be tough since we had classes during the summer in the PA program as well. But there was a week between spring and summer classes where I might be able to make the trip.

"You could bring someone with you," he suggested. "In fact, you should. It's the kind of experience you don't want to see on your own. You need backup to believe it's real. Do you know what I mean?"

"I'd be with you," I reminded him.

"Still. If you wanted to bring a friend. Or someone special."

At that moment, my phone finally buzzed with an incoming message. It was from Beckett. It was a drop point from the map, giving me his address. My heart fell. That was it? *He leaves with his ex-fiancee and this is all I get?* I forced myself to put the phone face down on the table and look up at my dad.

"He sent the address."

"Great."

Another message vibrated the phone on the table. I snatched it up, reading, *I'm sorry. Please come. I hope you haven't been worrying. I'm sorry.*

It wasn't enough. I wanted to know everything. I wanted to know he was okay. Still, it was better than just the map location. I stared at the screen a moment longer, than put it down.

My dad was watching me when I looked up. I frowned. "What?"

"Does he know?" he asked.

"Does who know what?"

"Your Beckett. Does he know how you feel?"

My heart stopped. I looked away. "I don't know what you mean."

"I think you do."

Unconsciously, I began to play with the bare spot on my left ring finger. "Dad. Don't be weird."

He sighed. "It's times like this I miss your mom the most. She would have known what to say."

"You don't have to say anything."

"I know that's what you'd prefer," he drawled, rolling his eyes in imitation of my younger self. "But sometimes you just have to put up with your old, decrepit dad giving you fatherly advice."

"Oh brother." My dad was anything but decrepit. But he always pulled this bullshit when he wanted to tell me what to do.

"One thing I've learned from your mother's passing is that life is too short."

It was too cliché to be his final advice. I waited.

"It's too short to waste on people who don't give as much as they get. And it's way too short to waste on not going after what you want because you're scared."

"Have you been listening to self-help books in your helmet speakers?"

"Har har. You are hilarious." He paused to take a long drink from his margarita. "My point is, I want the best for you. And I don't want you wasting your time on someone who will never return your feelings."

"And what about someone who does?" I asked.

"Then don't waste your time waiting around. Go get him." He paused. "Or her. I guess I should leave that possibility open, right? That's the way you youths are."

"Now who's hilarious?" I said dryly.

He ignored me, signaling the passing waitress for the check.

"I have something I want to give you," he said when she disappeared toward the cash register. He slipped his hand into his breast pocket and pulled out something small enough to fit in his fist. "I've carried these with me since your mom died. I wanted them to remind me of her, and remind me how lucky I was to have her. And now I've gotten lucky again with Charlene. In a different way, of course."

My stomach clenched, but I smiled.

He nodded. "But this is something that belongs to just us. You, me, and your mom. You were what made us us."

I knew what he meant. It was something my parents had told me my whole life. They weren't married when my mom got pregnant, and they didn't get married until after I was born. But they always said they didn't get married just because I came along. They said I made them want to be together in every possible way, including legally. That I made them them.

"That's never going to change. I want you to have it so you can remember that." He held his fist out, gesturing for me to cup my hand below his. When he opened his fingers, my mom's gold wedding rings fell into my hand.

Feelings of awe, joy, and sorrow washed over me. Tears sprang to my eyes again. I knew it wouldn't be a torrent, like it had been before, but I also knew there was no resisting these tears. I stirred the rings in my hand—the diamond solitaire and the curved band of aquamarine—my birthstone—that slipped around it.

My dad spoke softly when he continued, "I know you're not going to be married any time soon—"

I looked up, eyes wide.

But he suspected nothing, he was only talking. "And I wouldn't expect you to wear your mother's rings when—if—you get married. But I wanted you to have them. She'd like that."

I nodded, unable to speak. I wanted the rings, because they'd belonged to my mother. I didn't want the rings, because the only reason I had them was that my mother was dead. I wanted to confess everything to my father in a rush. Tell him I was already married and that I'd thought even though it was a lie at first, maybe it wasn't going to be a complete lie anymore and then we'd come here and everything was falling apart. But I didn't want to tell him any of it. I didn't want to break his heart to think that not only had his baby girl married without telling him, but that she'd done it for an apartment.

So I said nothing. I closed the rings in my fist and squeezed them until the stones bit into my skin. And I missed my mother so fiercely it was like a physical presence inside of me wanting to escape. My dad covered my fist with both of his palms.

"She'd be so proud of you."

I nodded. "Thank you."

The waitress returned with the little black folder for the check, and my dad released my hands to accept it.

"So," he said after he tossed some cash into the folder, "let's go see if your Beckett needs rescuing, eh?"

"He's not—" I wanted to say that he wasn't mine. It was an instinctive reaction to dad teasing. But the protest died in my mouth. Because just like stepping over a crack, or holding my breath past the graveyard, I refused to put the words out in the universe. I didn't want to jinx it.

My mother's rings were still in my hand, and now I tried them on my right ring finger. They fit. That felt like a safe place to keep them for now. It was nice to have a little piece of her with me. Maybe she'd bring me some courage.

If only I knew what kind of courage I was going to need.

26

IN THIS CORNER...

*W*e stopped to buy a bottle of wine to bring to Beckett's house. Mrs. Anderson might have said we didn't need to bring anything, but it felt weird to show up empty-handed.

By the time we arrived, I was deeply regretting my margarita. My stomach was doing a cha-cha to the beat of my racing heart. I tried very hard to keep up appearances, but I think my busy fingers and my intermittent deep breaths gave me away. My dad was kind enough to pretend he didn't notice.

The house was brightly lit in the early evening, with icicle lights strung along the eaves, and glowing luminaries along both sides of the driveway. There were a few other cars parked along their curb, giving the definite impression of a party underway. It seemed like a big house, even for the neighborhood, and for the first time I wondered if I was going to be horribly underdressed for the party. All I had were jeans and the emerald green blouse I'd planned to wear the next day.

Too late now.

As we approached, it was clear this was an open house. The double front doors stood open, with only the screens closed across the entrance. From inside, the sounds of music and people told us we definitely had the right address. A few people lingering in the foyer or nearby archways looked our way as we came in, but when they didn't recognize us, they went back to their conversations.

I hated this kind of thing, where you have to walk among a bunch of strangers, and you only know one or two people at an event. You spend the whole time looking for a familiar face and convincing yourself that they're not there and then you're going to be the idiot at the party with no one to talk to. My pulse jittered in my veins as we made our way deeper into the house.

Back in the kitchen, I spotted Mrs. Anderson and pointed her out to my dad. He approached and gave her the bottle of wine with effusive compliments about the house and thank yous for inviting us. She looked at me with an anxiety I couldn't understand.

"Is Beckett here?" I asked.

"I'm sure he's around here somewhere," she said with a smile that didn't reach her eyes.

I scanned the room, hoping to spot him, but he didn't seem to be in the kitchen. My dad was still talking to Mrs. Anderson, and the minute he mentioned Alaska, he caught the attention of another man who was standing nearby. This was my dad's magic power. He could find something in common with anyone in a matter of minutes and start a conversation. I hadn't inherited it from him.

After a few minutes of my restless shifting at his side, my dad interrupted himself and said, "Em, why don't you go find your friend? I'll be here if you're looking for me."

"Thank you." I wove through the gathered people, checking for Beckett. The party spilled out through a series of french doors onto a large patio, where there were yet more people chatting in groups. Beyond the patio, a pool glowed with underwater lights. A single figure stood near the edge of the water. She had her back turned to me, but I recognized Emily.

Well now what? She was the last person I wanted to see, but she might also be my best shot at finding Beckett.

I tried to act casual as I came up to the edge of the pool, leaving enough space between us that it wouldn't look like I thought we were friends, or that I was trying not to get too close. It was a failure. There is no such magic distance.

"Emily," I said. "Hi."

She looked at me. "Oh. Hi."

I wanted to ask about Beckett, but I couldn't pretend I didn't see her protective posture or the look on her face. She wasn't happy. "Um, are you okay?" I asked.

She let out a dry laugh. "I'm fine, thanks."

"You don't...look fine."

"Great." She raised one finger to her face, dabbing at the soft skin under her eyes.

"I'm sorry, I didn't mean it like that."

She turned to me. "I suppose you hate me?"

Not expecting that. I stumbled over myself trying to answer. "N-no, I—why would—why would you think that?"

"You took his side."

"I—well...I mean, he's my friend."

"No, I get it." She sighed, tightening her crossed arms. "But I'm guessing that means you wouldn't be willing to get him to talk to me?"

"Umm..."

"I knew he was mad, but I guess I just thought after a few months, he'd at least be—" She shook her head. "Does he at least talk about me?"

Almost never, I wanted to say. Instead, I gave a vague shake of my head and focused on a ripple on the pool's surface.

"Will you at least tell me if he's seeing someone?" She took a step closer. "It's okay. I promise I won't get upset. Actually, I'd be kind of happy."

I snapped my eyes away from the pool to stare at her. "You would?" Maybe I had completely misinterpreted this whole thing.

"Kind of." She sounded less confident now. "At least then he couldn't hold it against me."

I knew it. I had guessed she'd met someone new. "Did you get dumped?" I asked.

She winced. Normally, I'd feel bad that I'd made her do that, but I found I was a bit short on sympathy for Emily just now. "It didn't work out," she said.

"So you figured you'd just go back?"

Her expression went sheepish. "He was going to marry me," she said. "You don't just throw that away."

My jaw dropped. "Are you serious right now? Do you even hear what you're saying? You're the one who threw it all away in the first place!"

Her eyes flashed with anger for the first time. "You wouldn't understand. Beckett and I go back a lot longer than you've been around."

I splayed my hands in front of me as if to keep her away. "You do realize you completely screwed him over, right? Not just by calling off the wedding. He was supposed to move in to *married* student housing, and you disqualified him only *days* before move-in."

"I figured he would just get a roommate or something," she said weakly.

"It was a little more complicated than that." I glared at her. "Remember? *Married* student housing. You don't just get a roommate."

"So what happened?"

Uh oh. I don't know what I thought was going to happen if I went down this road, but it should have been fairly obvious that I was walking on thin ice. There was pretty much no move I could make here that wasn't dangerous. So I took the chicken's way out. "You'd have to ask Beckett."

Her eyes went up and toward the house, settling on a window on the second floor. Then without a word, she set off toward the house.

Fuckity-fuck-fuck. I scrambled for my phone, barely seeing the message from Beckett on the lock screen. There was no time for that. I called him, hurrying after Emily into the depths of the party. He picked up in the middle of the first ring.

"Emmy? Are you here?"

"Emily is coming to you. Right now. And I think she might have figured it out."

"What?" he demanded. "What are you talking about?"

"I didn't tell her, I swear." But the noise of the party was making it impossible to hear anything he said, or be sure if he could hear me. I clicked the phone off and shoved it in my pocket, focused solely on keeping Emily in my sights.

I saw her turn and begin jogging up a flight of steps. She was easy to follow from there. The second floor was all but deserted, and she knew exactly where she was going. I was just steps behind her when she stormed through a door at the end of the hall.

"Beckett?" Her voice was shrill with held-back tears. It was a tone I knew from my own voice. She was *not* happy.

"Where's Emmy?" Beckett asked.

I ran to the doorway, catching myself on the frame with both hands. A bedroom, I assumed Beckett's. He stood at the foot of the bed, his entire body tense and his phone pressed to his ear. When he saw me, he relaxed just a fraction, and tossed the phone down on the bed.

"Emmy," he said.

She turned around in surprise. "This is between me and Beckett. It's none of your business."

"There is nothing between you and me, Emily," he said. "Remember?"

"How can you even say that?" She whirled back to face him, forgetting about me for the moment. "I made one mistake. You can't forgive one mistake?"

I had to press my lips together to keep from blurting out that she'd called off the wedding because she met someone else. All that would do was hurt Beckett. But my fingers curled into fists at my sides. I could have strangled her.

"It wasn't one mistake," Beckett said. "You *planned* this. For months. You didn't tell me you'd pulled out of Middlesex. You didn't tell me you'd signed up for classes at Arizona again. You had *months* to tell me you were having doubts about getting married. But you didn't. You waited. You waited until the last minute."

"I was scared!" Emily protested.

"And you couldn't tell me any sooner?"

"I just needed some time."

"That's not how you treat someone you supposedly love. Someone you were supposedly planning to spend the rest of your life with."

"Look, I said I'm sorry. I was figuring some stuff out."

I scoffed, and her head snapped in my direction again. "What?" she snapped. "Why are you even here?"

"Figuring some stuff out?" I repeated, giving her a look.

"People get cold feet, okay?" Her angry expression softened as she turned back to Beckett. "I'm asking you for another chance."

Beckett shrugged. "Well, you're not getting one. I can't trust you anymore. You lied to me for months."

"I didn't lie!"

"Not telling me is the same as lying. It's calculating."

"Oh, really?" All the softness and pleading was out of her now. She put her hands on both hips. "Don't you think that's a little hypocritical of you?"

"What are you talking about?"

"Emmy told me what you did."

His face went white and he looked at me with wide eyes. I shook my head in small, tight denials. I didn't know what she was talking about. I had definitely not told her.

"Don't you think the university would like to know that they've got someone living in married student housing who isn't even married?"

Wow. I knew this was a disaster in the making, but I couldn't help being impressed that she'd managed to put even that much together from the little I'd said by the pool.

Beckett kept his eyes trained on me until I shook my head again. I wished like hell I could call a time out and give him an exact replay of my conversation with her.

"Are you seriously trying to threaten me?" he said.

"I'm just saying, I'd try to be a little more understanding about other people's…choices when you're hardly innocent yourself."

I couldn't keep quiet anymore. "You can't blackmail him into taking you back. That's sick. And why would you even want to?"

"You don't even know what you're talking about, Emily," Beckett said. "And it's not your damn business anyway. Nothing about me is your business anymore, okay?"

Now she got desperate again. "How can you just shut me out like that? You said you love me."

"Past tense," he said. "And honestly, now I'm not even sure I ever loved you."

She stepped back like he'd slapped her. "You—how can you—you bastard."

"Oh, I'm sorry, does that hurt your feelings?" He tilted his head in mock concern. "Sucks, doesn't it?"

Part of me was shocked at his callousness, but part of me wanted to laugh. He obviously had some anger to let out, and frankly, he deserved a chance to confront her.

When she didn't say anything, he went on. "You wanna know

the truth? When you called it off, I was devastated. But I figured out part of it was that I felt guilty, and you know why? Because I was relieved. Deep inside, I was happy that you'd called it off. Because I was only marrying you to satisfy your parents. And that's a pretty shitty reason to get married, don't you think?"

I couldn't help thinking that an apartment might be a worse reason.

"If it was so horrible, then why did you ask me in the first place?" she demanded.

"Because I didn't know any better."

This time, I flinched along with her. They might be the truth, but those words had to sting.

He dropped his head, staring at the floor while he took a deep breath. "I'm sorry, but it's the truth. I thought what we had was fine. That it was enough. But fine isn't enough for a whole life. It isn't even enough for a relationship." He raised his eyes. "I hope someday you find someone who makes you understand that."

Emily's lower lip trembled, and her brown eyes flashed. "Don't try to make yourself out to be the good guy here," she snapped. "What do you even know about it? Like you're some relationship expert? Like you know what I feel? You don't even know what you feel. I was always the one who was in charge in our relationship. You just did whatever I told you."

"Then why the hell would you want me back?" Beckett asked.

"Because it worked." She wagged her finger between the two of them in angry little jerks. "*We* worked."

"Maybe for you," he said tiredly.

"I gave you everything," she said. "I broke a promise to my father for you. And this is how you repay me?"

"Don't hide behind that. You didn't do anything you didn't want to do. Ever."

At that moment, I knew I shouldn't be standing there listening. I was already deeper into their relationship than I ever should have been. As much as I wanted to strangle Emily, she didn't deserve to have a spectator for this. I stepped back from the doorway and put my back to the wall where they wouldn't see me anymore. I should have left, I knew that. But the instinct to protect Beckett—and myself—was too strong. So I stayed, hating myself a little.

"You never respected my promise. You were always jealous that I put my father first."

"Are you kidding me with this? I wasn't jealous of your dad. That is so fucked up!"

"Would you stop swearing at me? You never used to be so foul-mouthed."

"Fucking Newsflash: I just didn't swear around you. Because it was what you fucking wanted."

On and on it went. Their voices and their accusations got more angry until I couldn't take it anymore and I slipped away from the door, hiding myself in a nearby bathroom. From there, it was hard to make out words, even though I could still hear the rise and fall. It was so hard to hear Beckett, who was usually so sweet-natured, be so unbending and furious. But I knew this was a fight that had been coming for months. He'd never had the chance to confront her. No contact since the last phone call he'd had with her on the deck at Ashley's house.

Eventually the voices got louder and I could hear their words once more as they moved into the hall.

"Get out. I'm over this. Go!"

"Don't you dare try to throw me out! I'm not going to let you humiliate me in front of all these people by making me leave. Your mother is going to be furious with you."

"I don't care! Go tell her. I don't give a shit!"

"Someday you'll realize I was the best thing that ever happened to you, and then you'll want me back, and I will laugh in your face."

"Never gonna happen."

Emily made an incoherent sound of rage. "Go to hell!"

"According to you, I'm already going there."

"You know, maybe I should just go ahead and tell Middlesex you're a fraud. It would serve you right if you got kicked out!"

"You immature little girl. You know what? Go ahead. I got receipts."

"What is that supposed to mean?"

"It means get out."

"I hope you're miserable for the rest of your life," she snapped.

"Sorry to disappoint you, but I've never been happier."

She made another wordless sound, but there was no other retort. She stormed off, heels clicking on the tile.

Once she was gone, I didn't know what to do. Did I throw open the door and yell surprise? Did I slowly slide it open so I didn't startle him? Or did I try not to let him know that I was listening in the whole time?

Beckett called out softly, "Emmy? Are you still up here?"

Grimacing, I slowly opened the door to find him still standing in the hall. "Here," I said, feeling guilty and about an inch tall.

"So...you heard all that?"

"Kind of."

He sighed. "I'm sorry. That wasn't...that wasn't the best person I've ever been."

"I think you needed to get some things off your chest."

"You think?"

I looked anxiously toward the stairs. "Do you think she's actually going to try to get you kicked out of our apartment?"

"She can't," he said. "We are actually married, remember?"

"But if she found that out..." I shuddered. "I don't think she'd keep it to herself."

"So I'd tell them first. I'll tell them right now if you want." He took two steps in the direction of the party.

"No!" I grabbed his arm. "You can't! My dad can't find out! It would break his heart."

"Well, then what do you want to do?"

"I don't know! I don't want her to tell anyone. I don't want anyone to know! Ever!"

His face fell. "Oh. Well. Okay then."

I couldn't tell what I'd done wrong, but I was too freaked out at the idea of Emily somehow outing me to my dad to give it much attention. I squeezed Beckett's hand. "I'm going to get my dad out of here, okay? It's just...it's too much. It's freaking me out."

"Sure."

"I'll see you at the airport tomorrow, okay? And I'll text you later." I leaned in and gave him a quick kiss on the cheek. "Merry Christmas."

THE DOWNWARD SPIRAL

*D*ownstairs, I found my dad still chatting with strangers. He had them all wrapped around his finger with an elaborate story about a flat tire in the middle of the Canadian Rockies. I quickly searched the house for any sign of Emily, but couldn't find her.

Please god, let her be gone. Let her try to preserve some dignity and leave without saying a word.

Still, it was probably for the best that I got him out of there. I didn't think it was outside the realm of possibility that Emily would decide to make a scene. So I waited for my dad to finish his story, then touched him on the elbow.

"You wanna head out?" I asked cheerfully.

He looked confused. "Are you sure?"

"Yeah, I thought maybe we could catch a movie or something."

"What is going on with you? You've been squirrelly since you got here."

"Dad, please?" I couldn't think of what else to say. I was counting on his inherent desire to do what I needed.

"Okay, baby girl. If you say so."

We Irish goodbyed it, slipping out without a word to anyone.

In the car, my dad didn't say anything for a long time, but I knew he would. It was just a question of when. We were almost back to the hotel when he couldn't stand it any longer.

"I take it he didn't need rescuing?"

"He rescued himself," I said to the window.

"You sure about that?"

"Yep. Dragon slayed." Assuming that Emily was the dragon in this scenario. And assuming she didn't carry out her idle threat.

"And did the heroine win the heart of the prince?"

"Metaphor's getting a little thin here, dad."

"Well, if our heroine needs some sage advice from her mentor, let me know."

Man, he really was trying to make up for his perceived failings. I gave him a little smile. "The heroine is fine, thanks."

Sorry I ran out so quick. I was freaking out.

You okay?

Emily didn't try again did she?

Beck? Emily isn't still there is she?

I'm getting a little nervous here with you not answering. Tell me Emily didn't come back.

I'm freaking out. She didn't figure it out, did she? PLEASE ANSWER

Can you just let me know you're okay?

Ok, I'm starting to worry about you.

Answer! You're making me crazy.

ANSWER ME ANSWER ME ANSWER ME ANSWER ME.

Why aren't you answering your phone?

Your battery better be dead. Or you phone better be in a toilet.

Beckett please!

Okay it's been like 8 hours and I haven't heard a word from you. I'm getting seriously pissed off. You better be tied up in a closet or something.

WTF BECKETT I AM GOING TO KILL YOU

ANSWER ME

THIS ISN'T FUNNY ANYMORE.

ANSWER ME!

I'M LEAVING FOR THE AIRPORT NOW AND I SWEAR TO GOD IF YOU'RE NOT THERE I AM CALLING THE POLICE.

To say I was mad after a night of barely sleeping and never hearing a word from Beckett would be to say that the Rocky Mountains are a little hilly.

I. Was. Furious.

And terrified, because I had absolutely no idea what might have happened to Beckett. Did Emily try to carry out her threat? Had she somehow found out the truth and come back to tell his family everything? Or had something truly horrible happened to him? What if he'd gone out for a walk to get away from his family and he'd been hit by a car? What if he'd gotten sick or hurt? What if Emily had come back and somehow convinced him to take her back after all? What if he'd chosen her over me?

But I had to keep it all locked up inside my head. I'd already getting my dad more involved in my drama than I should have. We had a nice breakfast together and exchanged gifts. I gave him a few extra credits for his audiobook subscription service. He gave me a silver chain and a ceramic pendant with an anatomical drawing of a heart on it. I loved it, and put it on immediately.

He gave me minimal shit about my constant need to check my phone. I tried to only send my increasingly enraged messages when he was distracted by the waitress or something.

We sat with our coffee for a while after the breakfast dishes were cleared. My internal monologue was something on the order of *pleasedon'tbringituppleasedon'tbringituppleasedon'tbringitup.* But I knew that kind of magical thinking was useless.

"Emmy, you've made it pretty clear that you don't want to talk about whatever it is that's going on with you right now." He held up a hand to stop me from protesting. "And that's okay. I don't need to know. And I've already given you more advice than you probably ever wanted. But I gotta tell you that I'm here for you, no matter what. You say the word, and I'll be there as soon as a plane can get me there. And if anyone ever hurts you, I'll kill him. No questions asked."

I couldn't help laughing. "You've been spending too much time with bikers. You're a computer geek, remember?"

"Well, then I'll hack his computer and ruin his life—or her life." He paused, finger raised. "Whatever you're into."

"Dad." I rolled my eyes.

"But he better be worth all this." He gestured to my phone, then me in general. "You deserve someone who loves the hell out of you, and doesn't make you feel like crap."

I did feel like crap right now, I had to admit.

"How did you know that mom was the one?" I asked.

He thought about it for longer than I expected. "She got me. From the very first time we met, I never felt like I had to be anything but myself with her." Then he grinned. "Plus, we weren't supposed to date coworkers at the company we worked for at the time. I figured if I was willing to break the rules for her, she was probably someone pretty special."

Then I asked a question that had always bugged me. "Didn't you ever feel forced? Because of me, I mean. Like you just convinced yourself you belonged together because you were stuck with me?"

My dad laughed. "Baby girl, trust me, nothing would have driven us apart faster than having a kid if we weren't meant to be. Maybe someday you'll have kids of your own—I kind of hope you do, honestly—and you'll see. Being a parent is the hardest thing in the world. Taking that on with someone you're not that into? That would only make it harder." He rubbed his eyes. "Now unfortunately, we gotta hit the road, or I'm going to miss my flight."

His flight was hours earlier than mine, so I had to say goodbye to him at the security gates for his terminal. We hugged.

He apologized for stranding me in the airport for hours. I told him it was fine. We hugged some more. He made me swear I'd come visit him in Alaska in the spring. I swore I would. We hugged some more. Finally, he got to the point in the line where I couldn't go any further with him and I said goodbye one last time, and walked away so I wouldn't have to watch anxiously for final glimpses of him before he disappeared through the body scanner.

Then I found myself the quietest corner I could and called Beckett.

The call went straight to his voice mail, and I took deep breaths while I listened to his outgoing message. The last thing I wanted to do was break down on a recording.

The beep told me it was time to speak.

"Beckett. It's Emmy. Look, I don't know why you won't answer me. I hope you're okay. I, um—" I paused to regroup when my voice cracked. "I just wanted to say that I understand if you changed your mind about us, or whatever, but can you at least have the decency to tell me? I thought I deserved at least that. We're supposed to be friends. And we're married. You can't just ghost me like this." Now that I was getting to the heart of it, my voice was stronger. And my anger was rising. "I'm a big girl. I can handle it if you feel like I was a mistake. But I cannot handle you ignoring me. How did you think that was going to work in Iowa? Were you just going to pretend I wasn't there when you got back to the apartment? Were you going to sneak all your stuff out in the middle of the night? What's the plan here, Beckett? Because I think I've at least earned some common decency. I'd think you'd at least treat me better than Emily treated you. So... so, if it's over, fucking man up and tell me it's over." My mouth worked without making any words for a minute while I tried to figure out how the hell to end a rant like this. "So, goodbye."

Pathetic.

LEAVING ON A JET PLANE

J took myself through security and arrived at my gate so early there were still another two flights to leave from it before mine began boarding. It was Christmas Day, so everyone was either wildly cheerful or inordinately grumpy. I fit right in with the second group.

All I wanted to do was call Ashley or Mary, preferably both, and spill my entire story to them. Everything that had happened since the idiotic decision to marry Beckett in Las Vegas. I needed their advice, and even more than that, their unwavering support. I knew they'd take my side. That's the kind of girlfriends they were. And I knew I'd been a terrible friend to them since I'd left California. With so many secrets to keep, I'd counted on avoidance to help me keep my mouth shut. But they'd take me in with no questions, no anger.

At least, I hoped they would.

Except it was Christmas. I couldn't interrupt their holidays.

The guilty pleasure reading I'd planned to do over the short break from school was suddenly too guilty. And I couldn't concentrate anyway. All I seemed capable of was slouching in an uncomfortable chair, staring blankly at the TV mounted near the ceiling. It was 24 Hours of *A Christmas Story*, and I had more than enough time to catch it at least twice. Yippee.

The flights to Orlando and Philadelphia left, taking their passengers with them until I was one of only a handful of people sitting at the gate. The clock was now officially ticking. Was Beckett going to show up for the flight? Or was he that much of a coward?

"Emmy."

Not a complete coward, I guess. I sat up and turned toward the sound of Beckett's voice. Seeing him brought up a blizzard of emotions. I was so relieved that he was apparently fine, and that he'd showed up. I was also confused, and not a little bit angry.

"Where the hell have you been?" I demanded, getting to my feet. "I have been calling and texting you all night. Why the hell haven't you answered me?!"

"I'm sorry," he said, "but—"

"You're sorry? I was worried sick. I thought you were dead. I thought Emily had come back and told your family everything. I thought you changed your mind and went back to her! And you didn't even have the decency to send me a single text message so I wouldn't freak out!" Tears escaped my burning eyes and trickled down my cheeks. "Nothing! Not a word!"

Beckett pulled his phone out of his pocket. "Someone hid my phone in the god damn mailbox on her way out of the house last night. Wanna guess who?"

The peak of my fury eroded slightly. "Are you kidding me?"

"I spent *hours* looking. Tore the house apart. Made my parents call everyone who was at the party to see if they took in on accident."

"Oh my god. How did you even find it?"

"Emily's mom called my mom this morning. Said Emily 'accidentally' took it with her when they left so she dropped it in the mailbox on her way out."

"Bullshit."

"You think?" He looked beyond annoyed. "The thing was completely dead when I found it. I only got to charge it on the car ride here, and I finally saw your messages. I'm so sorry, you have every right to be pissed."

"You couldn't call me from another phone? You didn't think I'd be worried sick about you? About what that psycho Emily might have done?"

His face turned red. "I...don't actually know your phone number."

"What the fuck, Beckett?" I demanded.

"Do you know mine?" he countered.

"It's four...eight?" I started, but then realized I couldn't remember the rest.

"Four-eight-oh," he prompted.

I tried very hard to conjure up the image of his Contact entry in my phone. His name always came up when he called or texted, never the number. I had no earthly idea.

"See?" Beckett cocked his head. "You put your name and number in my phone freshman year. I've never even dialed it."

"Still..." I crossed my arms. "You should have done *something*. I was worried!"

"Don't worry. Emily's not going to do anything," he said. "I will stay your dirty little secret, okay?" The bitterness in his voice surprised me.

"It's not that—well, okay, it was a little bit that—but I was freaked out that something happened to you, you idiot." I punched him softly in the shoulder. "And why didn't you call me as soon as your phone was charged?"

"I was in the car with my dad. And I was listening to your five voicemails, remember?"

I remembered. And now a tinge of fear swam through my stomach. What all had I said in that last voicemail? "Oh."

"Yeah." He looked down, rubbing the back of his head briefly. "I get that you were mad that I wasn't answering, but I guess I don't really get why you think *I'm* the one who would want to end…things. You're the one who doesn't want anyone to know about us."

"What?"

"You said it last night: 'I don't want anyone to know. Ever.'"

As soon as he said it, I remembered saying the words. "No!" I protested. "I didn't want anyone to know we got married in secret. My dad would be so crushed if he thought he wasn't at my wedding. That's all. Just the married part."

"Oh. I thought—I thought you meant me."

"No! I—" To my complete shock, the words "love you" had almost come out of my mouth.

What? When had that happened? My heart galloped as I scrambled for another way to end my thought. "You…you're…" I made a helpless gesture toward him. "I thought maybe you just needed a rebound, and I didn't want you to think that because we're married that you had to stay with me now."

We were probably providing some very interesting eaves-dropping for nearby passengers.

"So you were trying to give me an out?" he asked.

"Well, yeah. I don't want you to feel stuck. You've done stuck. I promised you an annulment, not another relationship you can't find your way out of."

"What if…what if I don't want an out?" Beck looked uncer-tain. "How would I convince you that you never make me feel stuck?"

"I guess you would tell me."

"And would you believe me?"

"I would want to." I blinked hard, trying not to let more tears escape. "And I would tell you I don't feel stuck either."

"Then I guess that would work out."

"Okay then." I looked at him, seeing my own confusion on his face. I had no idea where to go from here. There was more to be said, but where to begin? And was an airport even the place to talk about this? Frustration made my fingers curl into fists. I'd felt so close to him when arrived at this same airport. Just over 24 hours ago. How had everything gotten so messed up so fast? How could there be so much distance between us when we'd both just said we didn't want an out?

Beckett seemed lost in his own thoughts, but he suddenly grimaced, eyes squinted shut. Then he opened them and looked straight at me. "No, fuck it. I'm done dancing around this. Emmy, I'm in love with you."

"You are?"

"Yeah, and I'm sorry if that's too fucking much for you right now, but I didn't tell you how I felt when we met, and I didn't tell you how I felt when we got married, or when we fucking slept together, for god's sake, and that's just bullshit. I'm in fucking love with you, and I want to be with you, and you make me really god damn happy, and if it's just me, then I guess that's gonna have to be how it is, because I can't change it, and I'm really fucking tired of hiding it. I'm in love with you, okay?"

It was the most strident, swear-filled declaration of love that I could have imagined. It was perfectly Beckett. I burst into laughter.

"What?" he asked cautiously.

I rushed into him, wrapping my arms around his waist. I tilted my head back to look at him, and said, "I'm in love with you, too."

He smiled wide enough to make my heart melt before he kissed me. A perfect, movie-ending kiss for all the world to see. No secrets. Nothing fake. Just us.

∼

THAT NIGHT, we arrived at our humble little apartment. The spark that lit the flame between us. It felt more like coming home than ever before. There were kisses in the parking lot, in the lobby, and at the door. There was a trail of luggage, coats, and clothing that led from the front door to the bed. And then there was the two of us, together. Again, and more than before.

Later, Beckett retrieved the little velvet box from the corner of my underwear drawer and offered my ring to me.

"Emmy, I will annul the hell out of you if that's what you want, but will you wear this again for now, and be my wife for at least the rest of our lease?"

"Yes." I giggled, holding out my hand.

He slid it back onto my finger, and finally, my hand felt normal again. "If you play your cards right, maybe someday I'll give you a ring that didn't come from Walmart."

"Don't you dare. I love this ring."

He smiled and kissed my nose. "There you go, making me fall in love with you all over again."

"I better turn down the charm, or we'll never get that annulment."

"Would that be the worst thing in the world?"

My heart did a pirouette. "I think I could learn to live with it."

ONE YEAR LATER

Invitation, version 1, for family and pre-Iowa friends:
Together with their parents,
Emily Louise Black
and
Beckett Michael Anderson
request the honor of your presence
On their wedding day
Saturday, the Twenty-second of June
Eight o'clock in the evening

Invitation, version 2, for Iowa friends only.
DO NOT MIX UP THE LISTS:

Together with their parents,
Emily Louise Black
and
Beckett Michael Anderson
request the honor of your presence
As they renew their vows

Saturday, the Twenty-second of June
Eight o'clock in the evening
Shh! Remember, not everyone
knows they're already married!
Mum's the word!

ABOUT THE AUTHOR

ELLIE CAHILL is the not at all secret pen name of Young Adult author Liz Czukas. Ellie is the author of WHEN JOSS MET MATT, CALL ME MAYBE, and JUST A GIRL. She lives outside Milwaukee, WI with her family and the happiest golden retriever in the world.

Be the first to know when Ellie/Liz has a special offer or a new book you don't want to miss: Sign up for the newsletter!

elliecahill.com
elliecahillbooks@gmail.com

ALSO BY ELLIE CAHILL

When Joss Met Matt

Call Me, Maybe

Just a Girl

AS LIZ CZUKAS

Ask Again Later

Top Ten Clues You're Clueless

Throwing My Life Away

~

ACKNOWLEDGMENTS

Endless thank you's to the readers who give me something to do with all the stories in my head. You all make it worth getting up every day.

Extra thanks to:

Liz Lincoln, for speed reading and continued awesomeness.

My Hideaway Banditas for telling me I can and looking at images until they were cross-eyed.

Lisa and Amanda for insider info on Pathologists' Assistants. Any embarrassing errors are all on me, not these amazing women, who are also my dear friends, voracious readers who will step out of their comfort zones for me, and would totally be on my roller derby team if I had one.

Laura Bradford for continuing to be the agent with the mostest.

My family, especially Kiddo who let me work work work when he would have liked some attention.